I is for Indecent

Also by Alison Tyler

Best Bondage Erotica

Best Bondage Erotica 2

Exposed

Got a Minute?

The Happy Birthday Book of Erotica

Heat Wave: Sizzling Sex Stories

Hide & Seek (with Rachel Kramer Bussel)

Luscious: Stories of Anal Eroticism

The Merry XXXmas Book of Erotica

Naughty or Nice?

Red Hot Erotica

Slave to Love

Three-Way

Caught Looking (with Rachel Kramer Bussel)

A Is for Amour

B Is for Bondage

C Is for Coeds

D Is for Dress-Up

E Is for Exotic

F Is for Fetish

G Is for Games

H Is for Hardcore

J Is for Jealousy

K Is for Kinky

L Is for Leather

I IS FOR INDECENT

EROTIC STORIES

EDITED BY ALISON TYLER

Published in the United States by Cleis Press Inc., P.O. Box 14697, San Francisco, California 94114.

Printed in the United States.
Cover design: Scott Idleman
Text design: Karen Quigg
Cleis Press logo art: Juana Alicia
First Edition.
10 9 8 7 6 5 4 3 2 1

# Acknowledgments

I'm indebted to:

Adam Nevill

Felice Newman

Frédérique Delacoste

Kristina Lloyd

and SAM, always.

When the heart speaks, the mind finds it indecent to object.

—MILAN KUNDERA

Contents

INTRODUCTION

IS IT JUST ME, OR IS IT HOT IN HERE? I mean, as soon as I decided *I* was for *indecent* (as opposed to *ice cream* or *indigenous* or *isosceles*), things began to heat up considerably. Of course, the word *indecent* conjures different definitions for each individual. What's indecent to me may be just another Friday afternoon for somebody else.

Although surely not everyone's Friday involves a visit to a local swingers' club, like that indulged in by the couple in Rachel Kramer Bussel's "The Secret to a Happy Marriage":

I sucked in air between my teeth as Beth's fingers found the entrance to my sex. She stroked me there, so lightly I wanted to scream, playing with my wetness but not making any move to enter me. Katie's mouth got more intense, her lips fastening around my nipple ring and pulling upward while her other hand started lightly slapping at my other breast. I was panting by then, short, shallow, in-and-out breaths that pushed me closer to the edge of orgasm.

And I'm assuming that not everybody's routine Friday night features an impromptu fuck after public peeing as in Janine Ashbless's "Wet":

...without ceremony, he was suddenly inside me, nailing me to the wall.

Anyone could have come in and found us. Anyone could have glanced over the railings and watched.

"Dirty girl!" he repeated with a groan, his backside plunging under my hands. My wet hold-up stockings embraced his thighs. "What do you think you are? Wetting yourself in public!"

And perhaps I'm going out on a limb here, but my guess is that it's a rare Friday that finds your average John Doe playing dead for his twisted boyfriend, as the narrator does in Thomas S. Roche's wicked "Death Rock":

I lie still as he proceeds. I am always glad to feel the heat of his body and of his desire, excited to feel him inside me. But I do not move. I do not stir, not even an eyelash. I have spent months perfecting that; I find that the more I concentrate on remaining perfectly still, the more fervor Loren expresses. Loren is an excellent lover in these cases, I have to admit, and his knowledge of my body is intimate. He plays me like a cadaver flute. Or more accurately, a harmonica.

As you decide how to spice up your own next Friday night, check out these beauties. I've already found the fifteen indecent stories of my dreams.

XXX,
Alison

Janine Ashbless

Wet

I SHOULD HAVE GONE BEFORE we left the multiplex, but we were down two flights of escalators and out of the mall before I realized quite how full my bladder was.

"Ah. I need a pee."

My husband looked at me, his hand on the curve of my bum. "Can't it wait?"

"I'm busting."

He rolled his eyes. "Didn't you notice before we came out?"

I shrugged. The reason I hadn't noticed is that throughout the movie Terry had had his hand between my thighs, stroking the soft skin exposed above my hold-ups and teasing me through my panties. The picture had been one of those art-house dirty films that come out occasionally, the sort that nice middle-class couples go to because they wouldn't dare enter a porn theater: with professional actors but real sex, dressed up as ironic social commentary. It had filled my head with images I'd be replaying for weeks, and my knickers with a slippery wetness. Terry's gentle touches in the darkened auditorium had heightened my arousal to the point of delirium and taken my mind miles from other bodily needs. I hadn't noticed the fullness of my bladder while I was sitting. Not till now.

We returned past all the closed shops and rode the escalator back up to the cinema, but by the time we got there the place was locked up. Our late-night movie had been the last showing of the evening and the minimal staff hadn't hung round. "Oh, shit," I moaned.

"There's a toilet block on Corporation Street, isn't there?" said Terry.

"Is there?" I didn't know the city well; this wasn't our home territory. We'd only driven in for the movie. Normally we do all our shopping and work in the satellite town where we live.

"Well, there's definitely one back at the car park. Can you manage?"

I took a deep breath and nodded.

We rode back down through the deserted arcade. The shop windows tantalized with subdued lighting but the interiors were dark. I clenched my inner muscles and tried to distract myself by looking at what was on offer. This mall was quite upmarket, more so than the one at the base of the multistory in which we'd parked about half a mile away. Parking in the city was always awkward, even late at night.

There wasn't much traffic on the road as we emerged and it was easy to cross without waiting for the lights. Though the pubs were starting to shut the bars and clubs were still going strong, there wasn't a press of people on the pavements yet, nor any visible drunks. Walking was uncomfortable and I couldn't go at our usual speed. Terry took my hand sympathetically.

"You okay?"

I nodded, teeth gritted. "I shouldn't have had those glasses of wine before we came out."

"Or the coffee in the cinema."

I winced from the memory of the very large paper cup. "I didn't want to fall asleep."

"You think you would have?" His lips quirked wickedly. I grinned.

"I didn't know you were going to do that!"

"You liked it, though?"

I giggled, though only briefly because it was almost painful against the clenching of my muscles. "Couldn't you tell?"

"Dirty girl," he said softly. Reflected neon flashed on his gold-rimmed glasses as he tilted his head. Terry, who teaches physics, cultivates an intellectual look: disheveled sandy curls and an air of lofty academic detachment that verges on the cruel. I bet all the girls in his lectures at college fancy him. He makes me itch with lust even now we're respectably married. I flushed slightly, his glance almost enough to make me forget my predicament. Until we detoured through the ornate iron bollards closing off the pedestrianized Corporation Street, that is, and found that the toilet block in the middle was shut, according to an official notice, every night at 11:00 P.M.

"Bastards!" I whined, grabbing myself between the legs. In the shadow of the fake Georgian portico I just hoped I wasn't too visible. I ground my fingers against my clit. Terry's eyebrows rose.

"Does that help?"

"Uh...yeah." The pleasurable stimulation completely canceled out the more painful pressure of my bladder. "It sort of overrides the signals."

"Really?" He ran his hand across my distended lower belly and I nearly screamed, but then he tucked his fingertips into the crease between my thighs and I writhed against him. His long, cool fingers knew just what to do, rubbing in tight circles. "Better?"

"Yes." My voice came out in a squeak. "That's why I didn't notice in the cinema. It's all your fault."

He tutted. "*Mea culpa*. Well, we can't do this all the way home. Are you okay back to the car park? It's only five minutes."

I bit my lip. What choice did I have? "Let's go."

God, did it hurt when he let go. I held onto his arm for support as we made our way down the broad shopping avenues, dodging the other knots of nighttime walkers. I was nearly hobbling, and every time I stepped off a pavement the jolt seemed to go right through me. Terry stroked my hand reassuringly. I wanted him to talk and take my mind off things but he was unusually silent. Laughing, roughhousing youths spilled off a bus and swept around us but I couldn't even spare them enough attention to be faintly nervous as I would have been normally. My clothes felt clammy and my light summer skirt clung to my thighs.

We made it across the final road to the block concealing the multi-story car park. There were stairs up to the entrance and a wheelchair ramp, and both looked equally impassable to me. I stopped.

"I'm not sure I'm going to make it."

Terry turned to face me and pushed his hand between my legs to take a firm grip, making me moan with equal parts shock and gratitude.

"Get a room," suggested a passerby cheerily, but Terry ignored him.

"Hold it in," he ordered, rubbing my clit. "You're going to get there. Just hold it in."

Gasping, I nodded. My cheeks were flaming. At any other time it would have been with excitement at his daring.

"Do you want me to carry you?"

I shook my head and saw he understood; one squeeze and it would all be over.

"Okay." He coaxed me up the stairs one at a time, holding tight to my hand, and we passed into the ground-floor interior of the building. This was a shopping arcade too, but a cheaper one. The stores sold Tupperware and greetings cards and food you had to weigh out of tubs and everything-for-£1. They were shuttered but the concourse remained open all night because people were parked upstairs. They drifted through on their way back from pubs and restaurants and cinemas. It wasn't the sort of place I'd want to be on my own in the small hours.

"Oh, God," I whimpered under my breath.

"I'll go check if the toilets are open." Terry dropped my hand and trotted off before I could think to protest. I shuffled forward like a shopping-mall zombie, my thighs clenched and both fists balled at my hips. I felt like I had a fever; I was flushed with heat but plumes of chill kept washing up my spine. The shop fronts and the few passersby were a blur at the periphery of my vision.

Then came the first little sensation of warmth, and I realized I was leaking. I stopped, legs pressed, unable to take another step, utterly frantic. There were beads of sweat on my upper lip. "Terry!" I whimpered like a little lost girl.

And there he was, hurrying back to me, his face alight; nodding.

"Help me," I begged him, writhing. "Oh, please, Terry." Then my muscles finally gave way before the inevitable, and suddenly there was hot wetness all down my legs and I was pissing as I stood there on the tiled floor. The relief was indescribable, the agony transformed in a second into bliss, but the shame was indescribable, too. Tears ran down my face. I was shaking. Some part of me thought to try and save my new shoes so I opened my legs and let my water flood out. Other people were staring at me but I could hardly tell. I had eyes only for Terry who'd stopped a few paces off, transfixed. His pale eyes were wide like he'd never blink again as he watched me pee, staring at my crotch and my spread legs and the pool growing between my feet. I couldn't look down at myself but I could see his face, his expression of horror and awe.

Slowly, after an interminable period over which I had no control, the soft splashing grew still. I was empty. I shut my eyes. I felt Terry take my hands in his.

"Come on, love," he whispered. And he led me away in my wet knickers and stockings. He took me to the enclosed concrete stairwell that we'd descended earlier in the evening. I felt light-headed, almost drunk, with release. I thought we were going up to the car but he pulled me into the short corridor beneath the stairs, his grip on my wrist so tight it was uncomfortable. He pulled up my spattered skirt. "Get these off."

His hands tugged at my panties. Shuddering, I let him draw them down over my bum and my thighs and then I pulled the horrible reeking things off in a twisted wet knot. Terry flung them aside, then shoved me up against the cement wall. He was breathing hard.

"Dirty girl," he breathed. He grabbed my hand hard and forced it against his crotch, letting me find out for myself that he was so erect he was nudging out of the waistband of his trousers. Shaken and reeling, I was in no shape to do anything about it. He had to release it himself, with desperate clumsy movements. I stared aghast into his face; it was set and feral and almost unrecognizable. Then he pressed me back against the cold wall and hiked up my skirt even higher, pushing my feet apart with his own. His hand groped for my sex. It found pubic hair in wet ringlets and, deeper in, a hotter more viscid wetness that'd been in readiness for hours. Where his fingers went the blunt head of his cock followed, and without ceremony he was suddenly inside me, nailing me to the wall.

Anyone could have come in and found us. Anyone could have glanced over the railings and watched.

"Dirty girl!" he repeated with a groan, his backside plunging under my hands. My wet hold-up stockings embraced his thighs. "What do you think you are? Wetting yourself in public!"

My tears had earlier spilled out soundlessly; now I sobbed without tears. Each thrust wrenched another gasp from me. I understood his heat. Out there in front of everyone I'd given way helplessly to the most shameful biological imperative—and somehow the world had not come to an end. In fact the result had been relief so sweet that I was high from it, my head buzzing, my heart pounding. Now Terry's need was as urgent as mine had been, his inhibitions suddenly as trivial. I was his dirty girl. I was his girl who could piss my pants and weep in public and fuck with him in a stairwell where anyone might see, my groans loud and shameless, my need overwhelming everything, my dirty wet sex taking control of my body. And he—horny as hell for that wet slash, rampant and equally shameless—he was my dirty, dirty boy.

When we finally climbed the stairs we left my pee-soaked knickers lying on the floor for anyone to find. They were nice knickers, too; taupe silk and lace, bought for his birthday night out. I'd hoped when I put them on that he'd find them so provoking he'd have to play with me—I just hadn't expected to get them quite that wet.

LISETTE ASHTON

THAT MONDAY MORNING FEELING

IT WAS THE ONLY THING THAT MADE THE START of the working week bearable.

Mandy stepped out of the shower, her skin jeweled with beads of water and her pussy bare and tingling after enduring the closest of close shaves. She toweled herself quickly dry, conscious that there would only be time for one more cup of coffee before she left for the office.

Short black skirt.

Patent-leather black heels.

Low-cut white blouse.

Decaf.

And then she was out of the house, slamming the door closed and stepping onto the bus with the flavor of coffee beans still warming her mouth. Her hair was tied neatly back—ponytailed into a glossy length of raven tresses that fell between her shoulder blades. A small black purse completed the monochrome ensemble she always wore for the colorless experience of the office week. And Mandy savored the special thrill that came from being without bra or panties beneath her clothes on the Monday morning commute.

Not that being without underwear was the only thing that made the start of the working week bearable.

It was much more than that.

Standing room only on the bus meant she was jostled between an eclectic crowd of mature men in suits and yobbish youths in jeans and leathers. The scents of deodorant, aftershave, and sweat mingled like the headiest of erotic perfumes. Through the windows, the gray world outside was a drab and cheerless background to the journey. If not for the excitement of her adventure, Mandy would have thought the view bleak and depressing. At the first stop another queue of morning commuters climbed onto the bus. The crowded interior became more claustrophobic and cramped. Everyone shuffled closer together to make room for the newcomers.

Mandy pushed her rear against the groin of a thirty-something executive. She had noticed him standing behind her. His cheeks were dirtied by the sort of designer stubble that made her think of too much testosterone, men at the gym, and rugged movie stars playing the roles of escaped convicts. With only a glance at his face she knew that kissing him would leave her lips sore, scratched, and bruised and desperate for more. If they became lovers she imagined he would be hard, brutal, greedy, and demanding. His shoulders were broad inside his off-the-rail Armani clone. His vast physical presence towered over her as he clutched the safety strap descending from the bus's roof.

She squirmed her rear against him.

The thrust of his semisoft length pushed back.

Mandy shivered.

She knew she could have enjoyed a similar tactile thrill if she had been wearing panties beneath her skirt. Another layer of clothing would not have greatly hampered the sensation of the executive's concealed cock probing at her thinly veiled buttocks. But the decadence of being without underwear, and knowing that she was so close to sliding her bare sex against the stranger, was sufficient to make her temperature soar. Savoring the delicious frisson of his trousers gliding against her skirt, Mandy imagined she could hear the bristle of the fabrics as they slipped coarsely against each other. The grumble of the bus's engine was loud enough that she knew she couldn't really hear those sounds. There was a muted babble of conversation around her: loud enough to be deafening and low enough to be indecipherable. But, as the stranger's length thickened against her rear, she fancied herself aware of every minute detail.

She believed she could hear the sound of his suit scratching at her skirt. She believed she could smell the vital scent of his precome and the musky ripeness of her own, wet sex. Arousal knotted her stomach muscles. If she had glanced down at her chest, Mandy knew she would have seen the tips of her nipples jutting against the flimsy fabric of her blouse. But instead of looking down at herself, she kept her gaze fixed ahead as she subtly squirmed her backside against the executive.

He was fully hard.

The thrust of his erection pushed at her skirt. If not for the protective shield of his trousers, Mandy knew his throbbing cock could have slipped between her buttocks and pushed easily into her.

She rubbed more firmly against him, pretending she was moving with the sway of the bus, slyly shifting from side to side and writhing until she heard his soft, satisfied sigh.

The bus drew to a halt.

Without sparing a backward glance Mandy elbowed through the crowd of commuters and left the bus. She kept her gaze averted as the vehicle drove away, not caring if the executive was watching, not caring if he was intrigued, infatuated, or indifferent. It was enough to know that she had already made one man hard this morning. Her backside tingled pleasantly from where his erection had pressed against her. Her arousal was a strong and heady constant.

With the tube train due in mere moments, she had to rush away from the bus stop, into the underground station, and down three long escalator flights for the next stage of her journey.

The platform wasn't busy.

The air inside the underground station was arid and tasted of rust. The electric train throbbed like a pulse of charged sexuality. Mandy took a seat in a comparatively empty carriage. The only other occupant was a student in torn jeans and a Green Day T-shirt. Mandy sat opposite him and stretched as though she was still sleepy from the early start to the day.

Her blouse pulled tight across her chest.

She didn't need to glance down to know her nipples were jutting obviously against the thin fabric. The pressure against them was already sending delicious thrills through her body. Her cheeks were rouged with the blush of sexual excitement.

The Green Day student grinned.

With the skill of a practiced tease, Mandy avoided making eye contact. She rubbed the palm of her left hand down her sparsely clothed body, gliding her spread fingers from her breast, over her hip, and down to her bare knee. It was an exaggerated gesture of faux innocence. Mandy savored the sensation of caressing herself. Her left nipple was instantly ablaze. Her thigh bristled from the contact. Her skin was alive with a welter of greedy responses—tormented by her touch—and she was eager to suffer more.

From the corner of her eye Mandy noticed the student had pushed a hand against his crotch. His face was a grimace. He licked his lips with an obvious and impotent hunger.

Eager to be more daring, determined to give him a good show, Mandy glanced down at herself and then stroked the stiff bud of flesh that pushed at the fabric of her blouse.

The sensation was sublime.

She caught the stiff nipple between her finger and thumb and squeezed it gently. A crackle of arousal jolted her frame. Although she had known the pleasure would be intense she hadn't expected it to strike with such power and force.

She gasped. And then, as she moved her hand away, she glanced up and met the student's appreciative gaze. His eyes were wide. His fist was crushed into his lap. His jaw was clenched. He sat forward in his chair as though a more natural position was too uncomfortable to tolerate.

Feigning an embarrassed smile, Mandy stood up and walked past him.

"Sorry," she mumbled. "I hadn't noticed you sitting there."

While he was still fumbling to respond, trying to cover his lap with a notebook and mumbling something she didn't hear, the tube reached its station and Mandy hurried from the train to make her next stop on the underground.

Another tube.

A busier route.

The station on this platform was packed with commuters. Each passing train was filled to bursting with tightly compressed bodies. Mandy shivered excitedly at the thought of being crammed in amongst so many strangers. The eerily dry air of the underground stroked a languid caress against her bare sex. Every time a new train arrived at the platform it brought a warm, rushing breeze that was like the kiss of a lover's lips. She crushed her thighs together as the pleasure churned her stomach and made her briefly dizzy.

When she had neared the front of the queue for the approaching train a daring idea crossed her mind. The concept was so exciting she was almost too thrilled to act on it.

Another train thundered to the platform.

The doors of the train hissed open and she squeezed into the carriage, telling herself this was too great an opportunity to miss. She was standing with her back to the windows and the platform beyond. A substantial crowd remained, some of them glowering at the full train, most of them waiting with resigned patience, a few of them meeting Mandy's inquisitive gaze.

Mandy reached behind herself for the hem of her skirt and lifted it.

She continued to stare over her shoulder, watching for a response.

A dozen slack-jawed faces stared admiringly at the pert cheeks of her exposed backside. She could see eyes wide with appreciation and grins of raw, animal lust. If there had been the space to move aboard the train she would have bent forward and given her admiring audience a full view of her bare sex. If it hadn't been so cramped inside the train she would have bent forward and then stroked a finger between her labia so that all the waiting commuters could watch as she teased herself to an exhibitionist climax.

Then the train was speeding off.

Her audience disappeared as the train hurried into a tunnel.

And Mandy consoled herself with the knowledge that she had provided a brief flash of excitement to a good many morning travelers.

Alighting at the next stop, following the escalator up three flights and drinking in the cool morning air, she checked her wristwatch before walking over the road to the office building.

The lift was empty.

The clock above her office said she was ten minutes early.

And Mandy decided there was time to relieve herself of some of the tension she had been carrying before the humdrum routine of the working week had to begin. She settled herself into her cubicle and switched on the desktop machine that dominated her workspace. After a cursory glance around the mostly empty office, Mandy pressed both hands between her thighs.

It was nearly impossible to contain the sigh of contentment.

The pressure was so needed that the slightest touch of her hand almost brought her to a rush of satisfaction. The first two fingers of her left hand teased her lips apart. The first two fingers of her right chased languid circles against her clitoris. And as she listened to the faraway sounds of her workmates entering the room and taking their places inside the surrounding cubicles, Mandy casually stroked herself to climax.

It was not an earth-shattering orgasm. A puddle of moisture stained her seat. A scent of ripe musk perfumed the immediate air of her cubicle. Mandy sighed with satisfaction.

"Are you okay, Mandy?"

She glanced up and saw Becky's concerned face peering into her cubicle. The edge of the desk covered her bare sex and stained seat. A glance at the mirror she kept by her monitor told Mandy that her features looked flushed, but otherwise unremarkable. Nodding quickly, trying to conceal the naughty grin that wanted to split her lips, Mandy said, "I'm okay. The morning commute was just more demanding than I'd anticipated."

Becky rolled her eyes. In a sympathetic voice she said, "I've just spent an hour's journey getting ogled and touched up. There were two suits on the tube who couldn't keep their hands to themselves. There was one student on the bus who kept staring at my tits. And, in the lift up to this floor, I got my arse touched by that domineering bull dyke from accounts."

"Really?" Mandy gasped. "Which route do you take?"

As Becky explained the minutiae of her travel itinerary, Mandy memorized the details in readiness for her next Monday morning commute to the office. Privately, she thought it was the only thing that would make the start of the week bearable.

DONNA GEORGE STOREY

THE CUNT BOOK

I'D HAVE TO SAY JON CHOSE THE PERFECT MOMENT to tell us about the cunt book. The second pitcher of sangria was empty. So were the dinner plates, except for a few charred pieces of barbecued lake fish and slicks of vinaigrette shimmering in the light of the citronella candles.

We certainly needed a nudge to keep the fantasy going: that we'd invited Meg and Trevor over for their amusing rich-kid ennui, not because they were the only other people with a summer cottage on this end of the lake. That I was here as lady of the manor instead of the semisecret girlfriend of my nearly-divorced boss.

Jon even gave his story a title of sorts. "Let me tell you," he said, "about Uncle Jacques's Legacy."

Jon called him "Uncle Jacques," but he was really his father's childhood friend, a second-generation Frenchman with Cardinal Richelieu's nose and pockets full of caramels for Jon and his brothers. It was always an event when he came to dinner. Jon's mother worked in the kitchen for hours making odd foreign dishes, beef wrapped in pastry or stews that made the boys tipsy from the vapors alone. Uncle Jacques was what they used to call a confirmed bachelor—though he wasn't gay, Jon was very sure of that. His mother was always trying to fix him up with her unmarried friends: prim maiden ladies and pretty widows. Around Uncle Jacques, they giggled and touched their hair. But his mother's hopes always came to naught.

When Jon went to Paris his junior year of college, his parents insisted he visit Uncle Jacques in the Dordogne, where he'd retired to his ancestral village. Jon went for the free meal and stayed on for half a bottle of Sauternes—a golden liquid so sweet it made his mouth ache. Uncle Jacques was surprisingly easy to talk to for an old man. He admired Jon's camera, a Nikon F2, and confessed his own interest in the art of photography. Jon spouted some nonsense from an art course about the pursuit of ideal form and the challenge of conveying depth and suddenly, there in his hands was a photo album, the old-fashioned kind with thick black pages and a cord at the binding. He thought at first he might be required to ooh and ah over European landmarks, or worse yet, pictures of Uncle Jacques and his father as boys. But then he opened the book to the first page. What he saw took his breath away.

"What was it?" Meg was the first to bite.

"Art photos," Jon replied with unusual delicacy.

Trevor twisted his lips into an amiable prep school sneer. "He means pictures of naked women."

"Or parts of them," Jon corrected. "In extreme close-up. I wouldn't have guessed what it was at first, except for the fingers, holding the outer lips wide."

"It was a book of cunt pictures?" The sneer stretched into a cartoon leer.

"Yes. On one page," Jon said. "On the facing page was a formal portrait of a lady fully clothed. The kind you might see displayed on any mantelpiece. I'd guess from the hairstyles that some were from the forties and fifties. But others were recent, too. Girls my age."

"How decadent," Meg cooed. "Do you think he screwed them all?"

"I wondered that myself but didn't have the nerve to ask. He did tell me that since he had no son of his own, he wanted to pass the book on to me one day if I thought I might have use for it."

"Do you have it now?" Trevor's question had a hopeful lilt.

"No. Uncle Jacques must be over eighty, but he said in his last Christmas card he's feeling quite fit."

"I don't know if it was wise of him to make the offer," Trevor said. "Now he's got someone anxious for him to die."

"Who? You?" Meg asked with a grin.

I asked Jon if he recognized any of the faces. One of those maiden ladies or pretty widows?

Jon gave me an indulgent smile. "Frankly, I didn't pay much attention to the faces. What struck me was how different the women..."

Meg's Adirondack chair creaked. I saw Trevor's hand settle over her thigh.

"How different they looked *down there*," Jon continued. "Far more variety than you find on lips on a face. One was nearly fleshless, a slit peeking from a thicket of curls. The next was plump and meaty, almost prehensile. And then a Baroque extravaganza, folded and draped like swirls of rich cloth." He leaned back in the lounge chair and closed his eyes. "It's been thirty years, but I can still see those photographs."

We all gazed into the darkness as if we could see it, too—a woman's legs dropped open like butterfly wings and the secret, scarlet fruit within, suspended before our eyes in the summer night.

What was it that made me doubt him? The way he touched me between my legs as soon as we got into bed, murmuring satisfaction when he found me wet? Or, and this occurred to me as he cupped my breast and stroked the nipple with his thumb, was it the way that cunt book story put him so firmly back in charge, throwing Trevor off his game, making Meg squirm around on her little heart-shaped ass? He already knew my weakness for stories of his young, impressionable days—but surely he could do better than a libertine uncle who was, of all things, French?

I turned to face him. "Did your uncle really have a book like that?"

Without his glasses Jon's eyes looked smaller, the tender skin mapped with lines. He smiled.

"Do you really have an Uncle Jacques?"

His smile broadened. "Would I lie to you?"

He saved me from the answer with a kiss. In the year we'd been seeing each other, I'd become used to his evasions, about his wife, about his feelings for me. The price for sleeping with a man who was almost old enough to be my father.

Or my uncle.

If the story was real, there was so much I wanted to know. Did he get hard in front of the old man? Did he masturbate later that night in the guest bedroom, vintage vulvas fluttering through his head? Which picture did he see first when he took his cock in his hand? Or when he came, biting back his groans so Uncle Jacques wouldn't hear?

But he'd never tell me these things. I knew that. Jon's tongue was too clever, dancing lazily, darting in and out, feeding me a taste of the pleasures to come. Feeding me pictures, too, rising from the growing heat in my belly. Of a lady, lips glossed and softly parted, gazing heavenward as they always seemed to do in pictures back then. But down below she was hitching up her skirt, spreading her legs, half-teasing, half-shamed, to show her secret to that cool glass eye. She wanted it, even back then, when proper ladies didn't do such things. Or didn't tell. And I wanted it, too. I wanted it to be real.

I pulled away and lay back on the pillow. "Take my picture."

Jon looked at me blankly.

"Take my picture. Down there. Will you do it?"

In the dim light it was hard to read the play of expression on his face. But then he said: "Yes. I'd love to."

The next morning, we drove into town for the necessary supplies. The general store only had one roll of black-and-white film, verging on expiration. Jon fretted that he needed an umbrella reflector to get the lighting right—impossible to find in that outpost of civilization—though we did score a remnant of black velvet, dusty, but on sale at half price.

It seemed to take him forever to place the chaise lounge at the right angle to the window and drape the velvet properly, set up the tripod and take a light meter reading, while I waited in my beach robe rubbing my feet to keep them warm.

When he was finally ready, he gestured for me to undress and lie down. I shifted around to show off my best angles until I remembered it didn't matter where I placed my arms or if my breasts looked perky. I glanced down at my triangle of pubic hair, trimmed back for summer. Suddenly, it embarrassed me, at once too lush and somehow inadequate. Through the light brown curls I could see the indentation, like a thumbprint, where the groove began.

"Did they all have their legs open?" I asked.

Jon didn't seem to understand.

"The women in that book. I thought maybe some of them were shy and only let him get a glimpse."

We locked eyes for a moment. And then he did understand.

"Yes, I think there was one picture like that."

Click.

"Open your legs now, honey," he said gently. "We only have twenty-four shots on the roll."

The words slid deep into my belly, insistent as any cock. But when I started to spread my legs, my hips resisted, like rusty hinges. *Sit like a lady. Na, na, I can see your underwear.* Every childhood lesson about my body was tossed away in that first cool rush of air.

Click.

"A little wider."

I inched my knees to the edges of the chair. As if in sympathy, my mouth opened in a sigh.

John fumbled with the tripod and moved in closer, crouching. "Tilt up a bit."

Click.

A girlfriend in high school once told me to pretend the camera was my boyfriend. Look straight into the lens and whisper to yourself: *I love you, Mr. Camera*. Ashley was right, those pictures came out prettier. But what could a pussy do to be fetching? Pick up a dollar bill?

"Were any of those ladies…" I cleared my throat. "Were any of the ladies in the book touching themselves?"

I knew the answer before he said it.

"Yes, baby. Yes, they were."

I had to do it then, of course, had to slide my hand down and put a tentative finger on my clit, plump as a ripe berry. My thighs jerked open wider, quivering.

Click.

I began to strum.

Click.

Then do things I never did when I was alone. Rubbing my lips together then pulling them wide. Nipping my clit between two fingers when I pushed them together again.

Click.

"You're nice and swollen now. Try to push your lips out more. So I can see the hole." Jon's voice sounded hazy, as if he were calling to me from behind his office door.

I pushed.

"More. That's a good girl."

My flesh clicked, like the sound of a shutter closing.

"Beautiful."

A gush of wetness trickled down my slit onto the velvet.

"Oh," I cried involuntarily. "I've made a mess."

"Don't worry about it," Jon snapped. Then more kindly, "Show yourself to me. Show me how beautiful you are."

I pushed wider, my muscles aching sweetly with the strain. I wanted to show him. Not just him, but old Uncle Jacques, and a thousand unknown eyes. Then I felt it, down there between my legs, pulsing, as if the very air had taken on substance. It was so real I thought it was Jon, but he was still kneeling back at the tripod, hands on his camera. My finger found my clit again, jerking faster until I was practically clawing myself and sobbing with pleasure.

"Come for me, baby," Jon crooned. "I'll catch it for you and keep it right here."

A flurry of clicks, then the long, lazy purr of film rewinding.

For once he kept his promise.

Afterward, he came over and ran his fingers over the velvet beneath me. "You've made quite a puddle, haven't you?"

"Sorry about that."

He smiled and kissed my forehead. "Silly girl. You were terrific. May I make love to you now?" His tone was proper, almost Victorian, but there was no mistaking the hard-on in his jeans.

And so he took me there on the chair, pushing my knees up to my shoulders, eyes fixed at the place where our bodies joined and parted, using me the way a man uses a picture, for his pleasure alone.

We'd been back in the city a month when Jon handed me a package wrapped in pink paper with a cream satin bow. It was a photo album of fine leather.

I knew the story but was curious to see how it would unfold.

Looking, I saw things I'd never noticed in a few furtive glimpses of myself in a hand mirror. How the cowl of my clitoris veered to the left. How the inner lips flared out in petals, one slightly thicker. Each page revealed ever deeper layers, another smooth inner mouth and beyond, the rugged muscles of my vagina. Watching myself change and swell brought it all back—the vegetal smell of lake water, the softness of the velvet on my bare skin. I felt my cheeks flush. Such a naughty girl I was, turned on by pictures of my own pussy. Then I heard a click. I looked up, surprise on my face. Jon took a picture of that, too.

A year later, I ran into Meg at the gallery where I'd taken a job after Jon and I broke up. I would have left it at hellos, but she insisted we go for drinks. She told me Jon had come by himself to the lake that summer and that he seemed sad. Somehow that news didn't make me feel as good as I thought it would.

On the third drink, she got to the confession. I was the only person in the world she could tell. At the lake, she and Trevor had an awful fight and she ran to Jon for sympathy. They got roaring drunk and then she let him—well, actually, asked him to—take her picture. They didn't screw. Just pictures.

"You know," she said, "like that book he told us about."

"The cunt book? That was just some story Jon made up."

"No, I saw it. That old uncle must have finally died."

"Were there pictures of lots of different women?"

She shrugged. "It just looked like a bunch of pussies. I was pretty drunk."

"Faces, too?"

Meg peered into my face. For a moment I was sure she knew, but then she shook her head.

Relief made me generous. After another martini, I admitted I'd done it, too, and Meg seemed glad not to be alone. We even joked about starting a club, Uncle Jacques's Crazy Cunts, membership always open.

We both left the bar happy. For the first time in months, I felt good about that sorry little dream of my time with Jon.

I liked being part of a legacy.

RITA WINCHESTER

DADDY'S PILLOW

I HATE WHEN CHRISTIAN TRAVELS. I hate the big empty spot in my bed. I hate how I don't have to wrestle him for sheets and covers. I hate how cold I get without his warm body next to me. His pillow gives me comfort. I snuggle it close and inhale deeply. The smell of his skin and his aftershave are a ghostly presence, no matter how fresh the linens.

Unable to sleep, I roll over and stare at the place where he should be. Feel that clench in my belly. That loneliness that nibbles at my insides. I pull the pillow close, hold him, smell him. The phone rings.

"You awake?" I can hear the smile in his voice.

"I answered the phone," I laugh. I sniff again quietly; I don't want him to know my childish ways.

"Are you wrapped around my pillow?" His voice is soft, but I can tell by the tone that I am expected to answer honestly.

"Sort of."

"Don't you think you're a little old for comfort objects?"

"Maybe," I say. I draw the word out a little because I'm confused.

"Maybe you should be punished for being so flippant."

My shoulders go back of their own accord. My spine straightens. My cunt grows soft and warm and fluid. Now I am truly picking up the tone and I say, "Yes, Daddy."

"What shall we do to you, bad girl?"

My mind goes blank. I've never had phone sex. I've certainly never punished myself via telephone. "I don't know."

"Put me on speakerphone," he commands. I roll, releasing his pillow to hit the button, and settle the handset back in the base. When he speaks again, his voice booms in the room.

"Get the paddle. The short one. You know which one I mean."

I know. The one he has made me paddle myself with for his amusement, while he watched from the corner of the room, stroking his cock, not saying a word. I open the bedside table drawer and withdraw the short black paddle. It is fetchingly inscribed with the word *slut*. Delivered correctly and with enough patience, the word can be seen like a watermark on my skin.

"I have it," I say; my voice is trembling. I am wet and I am horny, and at the moment, I would give anything for him to be here. For him to be about to paddle my ass raw and then fuck me senseless.

"Ten on each side. I want them hard, Kelly, so I can hear them clearly. Twenty for humping my pillow while I'm gone."

I have never humped his pillow. Clutched at it, smelled it, cried on it—sure. But never humped it. But I don't complain. I say, "Twenty, Daddy," because I'm supposed to.

"Now position that gorgeous body over my pillow, stick your ass up in the air and make them loud. I want to hear. Go on."

His voice is so commanding I would swear that he is here in the room with me. I drape my torso over his pillow and his scent floats up at me. I shut my eyes and stick my ass up in the air. In my mind, I feel his hand coming down on my bare skin. A ribbon of moisture slides down my inner thigh. "Okay," I say and my voice is as soft as if he were right behind me.

I deliver the first blow and wonder if I am insane. Paddling my own ass at the directives of a man a thousand miles away. But he's not just a man, he is *my* man. And he's not just my man right now. He's Daddy and when he is Daddy, I do as he tells me.

"One!" I grunt and switch the paddle to the other hand to deliver blow two. Already my arms ache from the awkwardness. From the contortion. That pain adds to the fire on my bottom, and I feel my cunt twitch impatiently. This kind of pain signals reward. I wonder if that will be the case this time.

By blow ten, my arms are screaming and sweat has sheened my face, my chest. I am gritting my teeth and I hear his voice snake out at me. "Come on, now. Halfway there. Be a good girl and be strong. Keep going." I can tell by the husky sound in his voice that he's stroking his cock, touching himself. He is finding pleasure while I deliver pain to my own flesh. I am angry but at the same time I feel honored. And ready. I want to beg him to take the next plane home and fuck me. Bend me over and fuck me like an animal. He doesn't have to be nice or talk or even kiss me. All he has to do is shove his hard cock deep inside of me and fuck me until we are both mindless. That is all.

I don't say a word. I deliver blow eleven with a moan. A spasm settles in between my shoulder blades and I want to beg and cry. I continue with twelve, instead. When I reach eighteen, my eyes are leaking. I will not cry out, though. I am being punished. I must take my punishment like a good girl.

"Make the last two count," he growls. "Like I would if I were there."

His voice is low and he's panting. I close my eyes and conjure up the image of his big hand on his cock. How he strokes it. The reddish hair on his knuckles. The purple tip of his cock, the vein that runs down the back that I trace with my tongue. How flushed his hard-on gets when I call him by name. So I do. "Yes, Daddy."

Strokes nineteen and twenty leave my body locked. The flesh of my ass stings and I lie limp and I wait. I don't know what he'll do. We've never done this before. He will either hang up or direct me to my reward.

"Go back in the drawer and get the big blue one." He doesn't have to specify what he's talking about, I know exactly what he means.

I extract the vibrator. Eight inches in length, healthy girth. Three settings: low, medium, and nuclear.

"I assume you don't need lube," he laughs and I swear I can hear the rasping of the calluses on his palms gliding over the silky skin of his dick. I shake my head and catch myself.

"No. I don't need lube," I say in a small, quiet voice.

"Good girl. Lie down on your back with your head on my pillow and pull your legs up. Open them wide. Spread that beautiful cunt open for me."

I let out a groan at his words and do what he's asked. My back relaxes into the bed and the pain from my stiff muscles starts to lessen.

I pull my knees high and spread myself open, imagining he is here. Imagining he is standing in the corner, fisting his cock and watching me. My nipples spike and a shiver runs through me. His voice is like warm liquid on my skin.

"Now stick it in you, Kelly. Do it for Daddy."

I slide the vibrator deep inside of myself. My pussy opens willingly, embracing the rigid tool. I don't fuck myself yet. I don't turn it on. I wait for my command.

"Turn it on high."

I want to say I'm too sensitive for high. That the clit stimulator will make me crazy if I turn it on high. I stay silent, find the button, and depress it. The big blue vibrator jumps to life, nestled snugly all the way in my cunt. Tingly warmth shoots through me and I gasp.

Christian sighs and I hear, or imagine I hear, more sounds of his rough hand on himself. "Good girl. I can hear it. Does it feel good?"

I nod, remember and gasp, "Yes." Though I wish he would let me switch it to medium at least. At this speed it will be over far too quickly.

"I have a meeting in eight minutes," he says as if reading my mind and offering an explanation.

"O-kay," I breathe because already my insides are clutching and flickering around the toy. Already I am so close that little bursts of colored light are going off behind my eyelids.

"Now fuck yourself with it."

I start to move. Each thrust I accomplish buzzes my clit with intense pleasure. Each withdrawal massages my inner muscles. Each successful plunge tightens me to the point where all I want in the world is to come.

"Come with me, Kelly," he says, his words sliding into my ear. Burrowing under my skin.

I fuck faster, harder, with the blue silicone toy. In my mind's eye, it's Christian. Over me. In me. With that look on his face that says he owns me and loves to watch me come.

"Now, Kelly," he says. His voice is guttural. Not entirely the voice of a man. Part man, part animal.

My cunt milks at the vibrator as I cry out. I come and drink in the sounds of him coming with me, so many miles away from my body he might as well be on another planet. The moment the last echo of orgasm leaves me, I pray for him to tell me to shut off the vibrator. It's too intense. I feel like I might shatter into a thousand pieces.

"Turn it off, baby," he says. Again he has read my mind. Or my silence. One or the other.

I shut it off and wait, breathing hard, listening to him do the same.

"I have to go, baby."

"I miss you."

There is a smile in his voice. "Be a good girl and roll over and go back to sleep. It's too early to get up."

"Okay."

"What was that?" he asks. This time with mock severity. With a lovely warm laugh.

"Okay, Daddy," I say and I am smiling, too.

Then all I hear is the dial tone and my own heart beating.

LISABET SARAI

CROWD PLEASER

I LOVE NEW ORLEANS!" she sighed, stretching back luxuriously in the chaise on their Rue Royale balcony. Her partner did not reply; his mouth was delightfully busy between her thighs, lapping at the pungent juices that coated her folds and sending electric thrills up her spine.

At twilight, Rue Royale was not as busy as Bourbon Street, a block away. She could hear, faintly, the wail of a saxophone and the intermittent roar of a crowd. *Some girl taking off her top*, she thought with a satisfied smile, then moaned as her companion probed new depths with his tongue. There was no crowd here. Still, sightseers and revelers strolled by in twos and threes a few feet below them. Any one of them could look up and see her summer dress bunched around her waist, her diligent husband kneeling between her naked legs.

The exposure thrilled her; she knew that it had the same effect on him. "Eat me, baby," she murmured. "Make me come, right here where anyone could see."

He needed no additional encouragement. He grabbed her cheeks and opened her like ripe fruit, sucking hard at her wet, salty flesh. She writhed in his grasp, little gasps escaping her lips each time he raked his teeth over her engorged clit. "Oh, baby, yes, you know what I like, baby!"

Pausing briefly, he buried his nose in her curly muff. The scent drove him wild. "Let's see you, all of you," he said softly. In one motion, she stripped her dress over her head and let it fall. It floated through the curlicues of the ornamented railing, pale in the falling dusk, and onto the street below. If anyone had been passing, the wisp of clothing would have perhaps entangled itself on the stranger's head, leading him or her inexorably to look up. But at that moment, the road was empty.

Now she lay bare before him, her pert breasts, smooth belly, and creamy thighs framing that delicious dark cavern between them. He could not resist suckling the almond nipples that beckoned stiffly. His tongue traced down the hollow between her breasts, across her taut abdomen, and back to her sex, where he dabbled for a while, teasing her. He heard voices below them, the melodious accents of the French language. The French tongue, he thought with a grin, sweeping his from the back of her sex forward and ending with a flick to her center. She sighed and pressed her pelvis toward him.

Suddenly, he wanted more. "Get on your knees, babe," he whispered. "I can't stand it, I've got to fuck you."

Eagerly she obeyed, turning over on the chaise and raising her ass in the air. The yellow gaslights flickered on her skin. Drops of her own moisture glistened on her parted thighs. She reached back between them, stroking herself with two fingers. "I'm so hot, so wet, I can barely hold on," she moaned.

He ripped open his zipper. His cock sprang out, ready for action. Clearly she needed no preparation; he could see her dripping, smell her heat. He plunged himself to the hilt into her exquisitely constricted cunt. She humped herself against his hardness, moaning in time with his thrusts, twisting her hips as she tried to take him deeper.

It didn't take long. She wasn't the most beautiful or most voluptuous woman he had known, but her lascivious joy at being exposed to the world aroused him in a unique way. He wanted everyone to see his abandoned, horny wife, her asscheeks trembling with each thrust, crying out in animal lust as he plowed her.

Though she had both hands on the chaise now, to balance his force, he knew she didn't need any manual stimulation. Dimly, he heard voices and laughter below. He skewered her one last time, as deeply as he could, and let himself explode. As he did, he managed to whisper in her ear: "They're watching us, babe...."

Her climax took her like a whirlwind. She felt his cock inside her, still like stone, the single point upon which her universe turned. She swelled and burst, expanding beyond the confines of her flesh, floating in the mellow evening light. She felt the eyes feasting upon her nakedness, their shock and their desire. She felt embarrassed and aroused and gloriously free.

With the money they were spending on this trip, they could have bought both a new refrigerator and a dishwasher. Never mind. It was their fifth wedding anniversary, and they planned to celebrate in their own way. The tickets to the Super Bowl alone had cost over two hundred dollars apiece. "Money well spent, you'll see," he assured her with a grin as they savored their crawfish étouffée later that evening. They had showered and changed, but when he released his foot from his sandal and began exploring, his toes found damp nakedness between her legs.

The next day, they sat quietly in their seats, pretending to watch the game. Neither of them was much of a sports fan. She didn't even know which teams were competing. Every now and again, her husband would get a bit excited as some burly, broad-shouldered guy moved the ball close to the crossed sticks at one end of the field or the other. She would bring his attention back to where it belonged, firmly squeezing the erect cock hidden under the program in his lap. Her own sex was swollen and aching.

God, let halftime come soon, she prayed, closing her eyes and squeezing her thighs together.

There was supposed to be a concert at halftime, the Irish band U2. She wondered briefly what twisted media genius had arranged this strange marriage between professional football and rock and roll. She had heard that this Super Bowl was the single largest event in the history of television. Millions of people were watching, all over America, probably all over the world. She licked her lips.

Their tickets included field passes for the concert. As soon as the second quarter ended, they grabbed their blanket and made their way down to the field.

The crowd streamed toward the stage that was being rolled into center field. Nobody noticed the couple establishing themselves at one end, just under the goalposts. He spread the blanket ceremoniously. She knelt down on it, in front of him, and began unfastening his pants.

Of course, he was hard; she had kept him that way through the first half of the game, but even if that had not been true, being exposed this way would have brought him fully erect in seconds. Her lips gently encircled his cock, even as she pushed his pants down to bare his ass. He surged in her mouth, and she backed off a bit, licking and nibbling, allowing him to regain control.

He kicked off his trousers and unbuttoned his shirt while she sucked him. He wore no undergarments. Leaning over her, he unzipped the back of her dress. Her mouth released him just long enough for him to pull it over her head and toss it onto the blanket. Like him, she was bare beneath.

He let her suck him for a while longer, fondling her sweet breasts, listening to the music and the applause. Finally, he couldn't stand anymore. "My turn," he said, pushing her onto her back on the blanket and raising her thighs up over her head. Now her whole nether region was exposed. Delicately, he brushed the tip of one finger over her clit. Her whole body convulsed in response.

His own rear in the air, he kneeled and began to lick her in long, sensuous strokes, delighting in her writhing and her moans. "You look so nasty," he said. He had to speak loudly to be heard above the concert sounds. "Everyone can see, baby, everybody." The noise from the crowd swelled, as if in response to his words. "I'll bet you'd like me to screw your ass, my cock deep inside, wouldn't you, here on prime time television?" As if to emphasize his words, he wet his finger in her cunt and then slid it smoothly into her anus.

Her only answer was a moan. She gripped her thighs hard, holding them open for him. Her nails bit into her tender flesh, but she didn't notice. His finger worked her rear passage, that invasion simultaneously painful and thrilling. His tongue flicked rapidly over her clit, bringing her right to the edge. For a moment she knew nothing but the sensations. She even forgot where they were, forgot her own name, and his.

Then she heard the band, the song, one of her favorites. "She moves in mysterious ways," they sang, and she remembered it all. "Baby, I want to be on top," she cried. "Let me ride you!"

He flipped over and she mounted him, his cock finding no resistance as it slipped into her. He seemed larger and harder than he had ever been, and now she was in control. She rode him fiercely, knowing that in taking her own pleasure she was giving him his.

Her thighs straddled him as she rocked back and forth. He filled and completed her. Her back arched, her honey-brown hair cascading down to her waist. Her fingers found her nipples and twisted hard. She wanted more, more sensation, deeper penetration. They had found their rhythm now, and their bodies rose and fell in unison, their grunts and wails echoing across the field.

Echoing?

Simultaneously, they realized that the music had stopped. The crowd was silent. They felt hot lights on their skin, heard the roar of a helicopter coming from afar. The audience had finally noticed the other halftime show going on at the end of the field.

It was all they needed. "Come now, baby," she wailed, as she ground herself down on him. Her insides were flooded with his searing fluids.

A climax as hot as the spotlights burned through her body. Together they shook, then lay panting together on the ground, but only for a moment. All hell had broken loose, whistles and sirens, yelling and stomping feet. He scooped up their clothes, grabbed the blanket and threw it around her shoulders. "Time to split, babe." They raced toward the staff exit that she had found two days before when they first explored the possibilities.

In the utility closet, they clung to each other, laughing and trembling. He kissed her naked, sweaty shoulder, caressed her breasts, cupped her furred mound in his palm. She could feel him hardening once more against her thigh. "Happy anniversary, baby," she sighed, as his fingers found their way into her sex.

On the plane home the next day, they were a bit subdued. They held hands while they read the newspapers together. "Terrorists!" one columnist screamed. "Immoral spawn of Satan," accused another. They looked at each other, slightly chagrined.

When they switched planes in Chicago, though, they caught a grainy video of themselves being broadcast on CNN. She was hardly recognizable, that slender woman with her hair tangled around her, ferociously slamming her body down on that of her lover. Still, the images ignited them again. His hand surreptitiously groped her ass; she pressed herself back against the bulge in his groin.

The urbane commentator did not seem nearly as upset as the newspapers had been. In fact there was a distinct gleam in his eye. "This was definitely a Super Bowl to remember," he noted dryly. "A real crowd-pleaser."

They looked at each other and burst into laughter. Then suddenly a worried expression crossed her face. "What's the matter, hon?" he asked, stroking her hair affectionately.

"Well, I was just thinking," she replied. "Whatever are we going to do for our tenth?"

Michael Hemmingson

The Installation

I

IVY BARTER, AN AMERICAN STUDENT working on her PhD in cultural anthropology and postcolonial theory, woke up inside her London flat one day and realized she was broke, she was in trouble, and the only thing she had that could possibly save her resided between her legs. She was twenty-eight years old, pale and petite with very small breasts and skinny legs and raven-black, greasy hair, and she still wore braces because of her crooked teeth so people thought she was fifteen or so, and her passport was always scrutinized as being a fake when she went to a pub for a pint of Guinness, the only liquor she drank. Some of the men she met at the bars would give her money, but it was always ten or twenty pounds and that was nothing, really; quid to last for a day.... She needed more...much more. She was not a prostitute...but her rent was two months past due, her credit cards were over the limit, the electric company was going to shut off the lights, the U.S. government wasn't going to give her any more financial aid because she had not made progress on her thesis…she had no job and little in her checking account…so she had an idea. She placed an ad in the paper; the ad read: FEMALE WILL DO ANYTHING FOR £5,000.

II

"What I want you to do, dear, is masturbate in public," Edward Kaff told Ivy during their first meeting at his lavish house in the Whitechapel area, "in front of all my friends, colleagues, ex-lovers, business partners, enemies, critics, and curious onlookers. It will be part of an art exhibit, of course—a very snooty, very snitty, very uptight sort of exhibit that I want to put a bit of arse-kicking into. You, in fact, will be part of the exhibit, *you will be a work of art*, an installation lying there naked on the floor in front of everyone and diddling your clit for, oh, an hour, maybe an hour and a half."

"Okay," said Ivy.

"Have I lost you yet?"

"Not yet."

"I need a pretty girl, like you. Not a model, not someone so…perfect. Just a regular young lady like yourself. You are the sort of young lady I am, in fact, looking for. You're very pretty, as they say in the vernacular."

"Thank you."

"But…now I have to tell you the finale; this is a big art show and my sixtieth birthday party—the finale is I will get naked with you and, by the bye, fook the *fuque* out of you."

"Okay."

"In front of everyone."

"Okay."

"And I don't mean some wham-bam-thank-you-ma'am sort of deal. It will be a long, sweaty, *healthy* fuck. I may be an old man, but I'm in top shape and practice Tantric lovemaking techniques. Do you know what this is?"

"Is it like Feng Shui?"

"I can go on up to six to eight hours of straight pussy, ass, and mouth pounding and not ejaculate."

"Oh."

"How does that sound?"

"Sounds interesting."

"You don't have a problem with an old man like me?"

"No," Ivy said.

"After all, your ad said *anything*."

"And I meant it."

"So what do you say, first impression?" he asked.

"I think it's something to think about," she said.

"Go home and 'think' on it, pretty little thing," he said, "but I need an answer in the next day or so. The exhibit is in two weeks. If you don't want to, I need to find another young lady. If I have to, I'll hire a call girl. But I'd rather have…someone like you."

III

She called Edward Kaff and told him yes, she would take the job.

"Good," said Kaff. "Good. I have a simple contract ready for you to sign, half a page long, straight to the point. I'll pay you half upon signing—that's £2,500—and the other half will be paid upon completion of the art project. The rest, we need to discuss in person. When is good for you, dear?"

"Anytime. When is good for you, Mr. Kaff?"

"None of that mister stuff, girl, you can just call me Edward. Can you come to my house in, oh, three hours?" he asked. "We'll seal the deal then."

IV

Indeed, the contract was simple: at the art show, she would whack off for no less than an hour and no longer than two hours, using her hands and various dildos that would be provided; she would do this in front of the people there and she would not stop; then she would engage in up to, but not exceeding, five-to-eight hours of sexual intercourse with Edward Kaff: *basically a live sex show.*

She signed the form and Kaff handed her a check for £2,500.

She looked at the check and thought: *This will save my life.*

She could cash it and take off, go on the road, to Greece maybe, start her life anew somewhere, forget the past.

But a deal was a deal.

And she could use the other half.

What the hell, all she had to do was fuck this guy.

"Have you ever slept with a man my age?" he asked her.

"No," she said, getting annoyed, "I never have."

"We cannot go into this particular piece of art blind," he told her. "Like with any performance, we need to rehearse for the show. This is why I wanted to get started now. Do you understand?"

"I think, yes."

"Good. Get undressed."

She looked at him like he was a naughty uncle peeking in on his niece taking a shower.

"I need to see your body," he told her. "I'm sure it's quite nice, a pretty form in the buff; but you must get used to being naked, since that is how we will work together."

"I see," said Ivy, and she casually, mechanically removed her outer clothes, panties, and bra and stood in front of Edward, looking down at the floor, her hands in front of her crotch, goose bumps forming on her skin.

"Let me see your cunny," he said. "Let me see that thick bush."

She removed her hands.

"Nice," he said, nodding, "very nice."

"Thank you," she said softly.

"Turn around and let me see your arse."

She did so.

"Nice. Now reach around and spread your cheeks."

She did so.

"Nice. Not a virgin there, it seems."

Ivy started to get wet.

Her nipples were hard.

Thinking about that night at the frat house party was getting her excited.

She liked what she was feeling…however alien and odd it all was.

"Turn around, pretty girl, and look at me."

She did so.

"Look at me."

Ivy's eyes met his.

"You're not just a pretty girl," he said, "you're one sexy bird."

She smiled.

"Your nipples are hard, and I know it's just not the draft."

She stared at him.

"You like this," he said.

"Yes," she said.

"I want you to lie down on the couch over there," he said, "and masturbate for me."

She felt herself flush.

"It's what you'll be doing, and you need to practice."

"I *know* how to jill off," she said.

He laughed and said: "*Jill off*, I like that. Okay, show me."

She moved to the living room couch. It was white, it was big, and it was very comfortable—softer than her bed. She could just fall asleep on it.

"Keep your eyes open," Edward told her. "Look at me, look at the ceiling, look at your feet, or look at me, but don't close your eyes. When you do it at the gallery, your eyes will be open, you will look at the people looking at you, and you will make yourself come. You *can* make yourself come, can't you?"

"Of course I can," she said, fingering her clit.

"Go to town, baby," he said, "slip a couple fingers in..."

She did this. She looked at the ceiling and then she looked at him. He was standing far away, observing, touching himself between the legs, squeezing the penis inside his pants.

"Do it," he said, moving closer.

She was rubbing her pussy hard, her pussy was dripping wet, and she came...and came again....

She was breathing hard....

"Oh, fuck," she said, and she made herself come a third time.

"Good, good, I bloody knew you had it in you," Edward Kaff said.

He was stroking her hair. He was sitting next to her. He touched her neck, her tits, her belly.

"You have nice skin, nice sweat," he said. "It smells sweet...it smells so...what's the word I'm looking for...feminine."

She smiled.

"You will do this to yourself, at the show, and then I will come to you like this, I will touch you like this, and I will do this," and he reached down and gave her a kiss. It was just a peck. He gave her another kiss, his tongue in her mouth. They kissed and he reached down and slid a finger into her....

"Okay?" he said.

"Okay," she said.

"I'm going to eat your pussy now," he said.

"That sounds...okay," she said.

"I'm very good at it," Kaff said, and this was no boast. When he got between her legs and licked her pussy and her asshole for half an hour, she came three times. No boast at all. The man knew what to do with his tongue and two fingers.

He stood up and took his pants off. His cock stood up straight, long and thick and veined. She said she wanted to suck on it but he told her that wasn't necessary; he told her it was time to fuck. "I'm going to fuck that cunny of yours for a very long time," he said, "and you're going to love it."

V

Did she love it?

Well, she enjoyed it—she got off—the old man was a great fuck and let's face it: he was probably the best fuck she'd ever had. He kept going and going and she wondered how he was able to do that, what this "Tantric" stuff was all about. Maybe it was Viagra. But he fucked her for a good three hours and after her twentieth orgasm, she stopped counting. They did take a break, when they drank some water and moved from the couch to the upstairs bedroom.

"Suck my cock now," he said, and she did, tasting the strong taste of her cunt juice all over that fat dick.

And then he came. He came a lot.

"Wow," she said.

"Did you have a good time?" Kaff asked her.

Ivy admitted that she had.

"Good."

"Did you?" she asked him.

He said: "I always enjoy fucking women…especially young women like you."

"I bet you do," she said and smiled.

"So…I think we should rehearse this at least two or three more times before the show."

"Yeah," said Ivy, "me too."

VI

She went to the bank and deposited the check.

Her pussy was wounded so she knew she'd have to wait a day or two before more action. She didn't want to call him; she didn't want to appear overanxious, eager, or horny—this whole matter was wrong, illicit, odd, not the sort of thing normal people engaged in when it came to sex, money, and the refuge of art.

She paid all her bills, paid rent for two months in advance, bought a lot of groceries, and rented some movies to watch.

Three days later, Kaff called. "You should come over," he said.

VII

And so the big night finally came. "Are you ready?" Kaff asked Ivy and she said: "As ready as I'll ever be."

"Then let's put on a show they'll never forget," said Kaff, giving her a light kiss on the cheek.

The gallery was located in central London on Charing Cross Road. It was a big place with three levels and on every wall was a painting by none other than Edward Kaff himself. Ivy didn't know much about art, but what she saw seemed okay—a lot of it was violent and sexual and, well, weird. Everyone attending looked rich and cultured; there were about one hundred people and they were well dressed, of all ages, and mingling about drinking imported champagne and talking and laughing and looking at each other and, Ivy assumed, gossiping. She was glad she didn't have to be around them; they were from a different world and they weren't the kind of people she would ever want to know. She was here to do a job and get the rest of her quid. She had entered the gallery completely naked, holding a bag of assorted sex toys. Needless to say, without a doubt, and completely according to Edward Kaff's plan, all chatter stopped, jaws dropped, and eyes widened as Ivy made her way though the people in the splendor of her skin.

"Ladies and gentlemen," announced Kaff, wearing a tuxedo and looking rather dapper, "may I present to you—*my slut!*"

No one knew what to make of this.

Ivy walked over to a large beanbag that was placed in the center of the gallery. She lay on her back, spread her legs, closed her eyes, and went to work with her hand.

She could feel all the eyes on her, the heat of bodies closing in, the warmth of the lights…mumbles, confusion, fascination, one woman saying, "She has a small and pretty pussy."

"Fear not!" said Kaff, "for this is all part of the show. This young trollop, this lover of mine, this comely little whore who loves to diddle—*she is my new canvas, my finest work of art, my erotic masterpiece!*"

Hearing his voice…doing this…the people around her…the excitement of the strange…it made Ivy come, and she was quite vocal about it.

Scattered applause.

"You see," said Kaff, "magnificent!"

She reached into the bag and took out the first sex toy—a small dildo.

She peeked through lowered eyelids: so many faces and eyes watching her with blasé interest…

"And now," said Kaff, "I shall read a very long poem. If you get bored, have a drink, have a finger food, watch the girl jill off…it is all part of the show."

He read his poem, which took about an hour. She half listened to it, paying more attention to her pussy and making herself come, going from the small dildo to the bigger one and to an even bigger one, as well as a butt plug...fucking herself with the rubber cocks as Kaff read his words that were filled with images of Europe and travel and vampires and music and Russia. What it all meant, she had no idea. She was no longer concerned with the people watching her...it didn't take long for most of them to become bored and go back to mingling, whispering, and drinking....

When Kaff was done reading, he went to her, joined her, touched her, kissed her, put his mouth to her vagina...

"More avant-garde theater, Eddie?" someone asked with an appropriate amount of sarcasm.

"You haven't seen nothing yet," he replied.

He undressed, and began to fuck her...

VIII

...and fucked and fucked for many hours like planned and promised and practiced. Most people got bored and left.

Then it was over.

"And so my latest art installation ends," said Kaff.

Rachel Kramer Bussel

The Secret to a Happy Marriage

IF PEOPLE ASK ME WHY I ALWAYS SEEM to have a smile on my face, glowing skin, and a spring in my step, I simply wink and toss off something about a healthy diet and plenty of exercise. Rarely, do I divulge the real secret to my rosy cheeks and bouncy personality, and even more rarely do I let on why my husband Larry and I have had such a long and happy marriage. Somehow, for a mother of two who lives in the suburbs, who's part of her Neighborhood Watch and bakes cookies every weekend, it just wouldn't be seemly to let everyone know that the extra-special ingredient to my recipe for long-term bliss is to mix things up in the bedroom. And by that I don't just mean adding a sex toy here or pair of crotchless panties there, though we get up to plenty of naughty play behind closed doors.

No, what I mean is that once a month, like clockwork, Larry and I visit our local swingers' club. There, we let loose, living out every fantasy we've ever had and some that only occur to us on the spot. At the club, I've been spanked, flogged, bound, and gagged. I've eaten pussy, shared cocksucking duty, been filmed doing fire play, gotten double-teamed while my wrists were tied behind my back, and come so hard I've screamed out loud, all while my husband watches. Our only rule is that when we go there, we don't fuck or play with each other. We share enough adventures together at home, so what makes it fun is for us to seek out new partners, or sometimes old ones, who really turn us on. I love watching him with his mouth buried between another woman's legs, lost in the exquisite ecstasy of tasting her juices. Sometimes another woman sucks his dick while he does so, but most of the time, I only catch the tail end, because I'm so busy having my own fun.

Last weekend was particularly memorable. One of the most popular couples who frequent the club are Beth and Katie. In their early twenties, they'd turn heads even if they weren't a couple, but when they're walking around naked or simply wearing skimpy G-strings, stopping every few seconds to make out, you can imagine they make countless dicks hard and pussies wet pretty much spontaneously. They're complete exhibitionists and always wind up going above and beyond the call of naked duty. They won't just tie each other up and fuck; they'll use gorgeous, expensive silky red rope, with Beth, the more dominant of the pair, running it between Katie's pussy lips and making her breasts pop out. When Beth sucks on Katie's nipples, she makes sure to grab one between her teeth and tug, or twist a nub between her fingers and twirl it around and around so anyone looking on can get the full effect. One time they set up a little corner "booth," where they took turns bending over for anyone who chose to spank them with their choice of implements. They bring a huge toy bag that sometimes has a video camera, and they've been known to get someone to tape them fucking, then gift the cameraman or woman with the tape, like a naughty goodie bag prize.

Sometimes they are incredible teases, choosing only to entwine their bodies against each other while everyone else looks on lustfully. Even the women who swear up and down they only love cock get horny when they see Beth and Katie. They're so truly tender to each other even amidst the wildest sex acts. One time, Beth kissed Katie passionately while she was sandwiched between two guys, one's cock in her pussy, one in her ass. Beth tends to prefer girls but Katie's more of the wild child, and neither seems to ever get jealous.

Larry's told me that he's jerked off to the idea of the two of them having their way with him, tying him up and gagging him, then taking turns sitting on his cock for mere moments, enough to keep him rock hard but unable to get off as they play musical chairs in front of him. We've certainly fantasized about the girls countless times in bed. I've always said that I wanted to lick both their pussies at once. I've watched them get head and heard their cries from clear across the room, lost with envy over the lucky tongue that got to be slammed inside those delicious lips.

The main thing to know about Beth and Katie is that they never accept come-ons; they always have to be the aggressors, the ones inviting others into their private erotic dance. Last weekend, I got my chance. The girls were particularly impressed with my new nipple rings, twin silver ovals with little beads on the ends that Larry had bought me for our anniversary. I'd been letting the piercings heal, and last time had kept my top on, creating an air of mystery. Some had thought I'd gotten my boobs done, while others picked sunburn as the cause for my sudden bashfulness. I just kept them guessing, and at home savored Larry's teeth tugging on the hoops when I was finally allowed to utilize them to full effect. Now, they were making their public debut, to much applause and public speculation. My nipples had never been as sensitive as they were now, and when Katie giggled and said she wanted to taste my new toys for herself, I smiled and said, "Be my guest." Really *I* was *her* guest, a visitor to her glorious lesbian playground as Beth stood behind me, letting me lean my head back onto her shoulder while she kissed the nape of my neck and whispered in my ear about what a dirty girl I was. Her words themselves weren't anything special, but coming from her lips, with her bare breasts pressed against my back, they almost made my knees buckle.

And Katie, who I'd thought of as mostly a bottom, pounced on my rings like they were candy. I reached behind me, gripping Beth's hips as she bit into my neck while Katie stared up at me as she took one ring between her teeth and began tugging.

"Oh, yeah, I like that," I said, staring back at Katie, hoping my husband was watching every second. My nipples were on fire, as were my cheeks, flaming bright red I was sure. I'd been watched before, but when I dared draw my gaze from Katie's wicked mouth, I saw many familiar faces glued on me, most of them with accompanying hands jerking on cocks or sliding along slick pussies.

"How's Katie doing, Angela?" Beth asked, her fingers finding ways to pinch my back, my stomach, my ass.

Katie's tongue slithered out to lick my hard pink flesh, flicking at the ring in the process. I watched her lap at one nipple while her other hand twisted my areola. "Perfect," I sighed, then sucked in air between my teeth as Beth's fingers found the entrance to my sex. She stroked me there, so lightly I wanted to scream, playing with my wetness but not making any move to enter me. Katie's mouth got more intense, her lips fastening around the ring and pulling upward while her other hand started lightly slapping at my other breast. I was panting by then, short, shallow, in-and-out breaths that pushed me closer to the edge of orgasm.

They kept me there at that high peak, but neither tried to push me over. Abruptly, Beth slithered out from behind me, forcing me to stand up straight, and pulled her girlfriend away. I saw them whispering, then looked down and saw my erect nipples with their adornments hanging perfectly off each end. I heard a laugh from Katie's lips and stood up straighter.

"We don't think you're quite ready to get fucked," said Beth. "Do you?"

It was a trick question if ever there was one, because I was so beyond ready to get fucked. "Your wish is my command," I said to Beth, because it was the truth. Tonight, she knew what was best for me, more than I or Larry or anyone else in the horny room.

"Good. Then shut your eyes," she instructed. The next thing I knew, a blindfold was placed over them. "Turn around and put your hands over your head." I did as she said, feeling my pussy tighten as I followed her order. Then hands were pushing me hard against the wall.

My pierced nipples met the hard, flat surface, the zing of pain racing through my body before settling into a dull throb.

"Spread your legs," came Beth's next order. I did, only to feel them spread further for me by her hands. Then someone was between my legs, pinching my labia. I'd never really thought of my pussy lips as sources of sexual pleasure; that was for my clit, and for inside. But soon something was being clamped to each lip, toward the top, near my clit. I heard a tinkling, like bells, then laughter. "Now if you move, your pussy's going to jingle," said Beth, raking her clawlike nails down the back of my neck. I shuddered, and sure enough, the bells hanging from my cunt gave off their own sound. "Those are really meant to go on a girl's nipples, but yours are otherwise occupied," said Beth.

"But that's just the beginning."

Because of the blindfold, all my senses were focused on what I could hear and feel, along with the anticipation of what mysterious torture awaited me. I found out very soon, when the stroke of a flogger struck my upper back, hard. Normally, it wouldn't have hurt so much as thudded, like an extrastrong backrub, but because of the heat emanating from my nipples, the pressure of the flogger pushed me further against the wall. Then, a pause, and something struck my ass. It was sharp and focused, and felt like a riding crop. I trembled, then whimpered. The crop made my pussy tingle.

Then came both the flogger and crop at once, one pounding deep into my upper back, one sizzling against my ass. I knew both women were lashing out at me, and was sure that anyone who hadn't been watching before was doing so now. The blows against my back were loud, drowning out my whimpers as the heat in my chest suffused my body. The crop and the clamps on my labia were what really pushed me over the edge. "Yes," I cried out loudly, as the instruments barreled against my skin. They kept striking me over and over until my whole body tingled like you do when you've just come into a warm room from a freezing outdoor day, only feeling on the edge of orgasm as well.

Then the room was still, and it felt to me like everyone was holding his or her breath, waiting, like me, to see what would happen next. One of the women (my money was on Beth) took the crop and began tapping it against my sex. Lightly at first, the leather hit my slit, sometimes striking the bells. Then it came harder, and I banged my fists against the wall, so horny I could scream. "Yeah," I heard behind me, then there were fingers tangled in my hair, fingers being shoved in my mouth, who knows how many hands on me, all touching and stroking and hitting me at once. When someone finally got around to fucking me with a huge dildo that stretched my pussy deliciously, I shuddered, my body craving every last inch of it. As I got mauled, I melted into my tormenters, my lovers, myself. I gave everything I had to my scene, and got back in return an orgasm that seemed to last for hours. Long after we left the club, my pussy pulsed with that special feeling only a rock-your-world climax can bring.

Beth and Katie took me into the bathroom and wiped me down, kissing and licking any sore spots and telling me that ours was the hottest scene they'd ever had at the club. I don't know if they were telling the truth, but for me, they gave my weekend, okay, my year, something to truly remember.

And that's my secret, one I'm happy to share if it'll help one lucky lady unlock her own erotic dreams, as naughty as they may be. We've all got them, those yearnings that don't simply go away because you've got a ring on your finger. I prefer to indulge my indecent thoughts, and will continue to do so, with a smile on my face.

TSAURAH LITZKY

GUILT

I DON'T WANT TO TELL MY FRIENDS I am having an affair with a priest. It's not that I'm ashamed; no way. It's more that my adventures between the sheets with Father Sal move me so deeply I don't want to talk about them.

I don't want to sit with Ursula and Carri at Southside Lounge drinking margaritas and talking affectionately about him. I don't want to tell them about the faded blue boxer shorts decorated with little Snoopys that he wears, nor do I want to tell my friends how much his hairy barrel chest turns me on.

I don't want to chat about his mighty eminence, so thick when it is erect and wanting me that it fills my palm. I especially don't want to get all girly-girl with my dear gal pals and giggle with them about the fact that Father's favorite position is indeed missionary. Nor do I wish to share with them the fact that due to the particularly fortunate geometry of our bodies, I can swing my legs up, up so that my toes can tickle the back of his neck while he is nailing me. Then, by just lifting my head a little bit, I can grab one of his nipples in my mouth and suck it so it gets as hard as the blessed cock that is reaming me. Most of all, I don't want to tell my friends that I think I am falling in love with him.

He visits me on Thursday evenings because that is the night when he is free of responsibilities for his parish. The day before his visits, I can't get him out of my mind. I anticipate how I will welcome him with a big juicy kiss and a nice glass of scotch, and my pussy gets so wet that the crotch of my panties is soaked.

I wonder how much falling in love with a priest will complicate my already complicated life. I can't imagine bringing him to the annual Passover Seder my eighty-nine-year-old aunt holds in her house out in Valley Stream, Long Island, but then I don't even have to bring him. Ours can be a secret love. People can be secret lovers for a long time. Last year, Carri's father died, and only three months later her mother married his best friend, Herbert. It turns out the mother and Herbert had been secret lovers for forty-five years. Lately, I have started to imagine Father Sal and me growing old together in our secret way. He will keep a pair of slippers at my house; I will always have a tube of Bengay around because even now he complains that his back sometimes aches after he fucks me. However, last night something happened that has made me worry about our future together. He and I may be developing a serious problem.

Sal always brings me roses, roses in different colors. Last night they were pink, the color of romance. He has also started to bring newspaper articles for us to discuss because, he says, he wants our time together to be about more than just the bed.

Last night, he brought over an article about Social Security reform. I poured him a hearty scotch and for me, white wine. Then I sat on his lap while we discussed the threats to the Social Security system. I couldn't resist putting my hand down between his legs to rest on his balls. I stoked them with adoring fingers. Very soon, his manly nature rose up and started smacking against my wrist like a wooden ruler. If this was punishment for me being a bad girl, I could take it and I wanted more.

Just as I was talking about the dangers of privatization, and comparing our system to retirement programs in Europe, my dear Sal suddenly picked me up out of my chair. Then he threw me over his shoulder like I was a sack of Bibles, carried me into the bedroom, and dumped me on the bed.

He was so impatient he did not even bother to undress me. There must have been something about the pension system in Holland that really turned him on. He just pulled up my skirt. I wasn't wearing panties—when he is around I like to offer not even the flimsiest impediment to him entering me. Then he unzipped his trousers and pulled out his proud piece. He sheathed it with the condom he always carries in his shirt pocket in anticipation of our raunchy romps. A second later, he pulled me onto my hands and knees and took me doggy style. With each deep lunge, his hot balls spanked my ass-cheeks, making me even more excited, so excited I wanted to privatize him for myself forever. He collapsed on top of me, his mouth sucking my neck, his scepter ramming into me, his sizable belly slapping my back like a silken cushion. Finally, he shot a steaming jet of pure heaven into me sending us both to kingdom come.

Then, as he usually did, Father Sal peeled off the condom and put it on my bedside table. He cocooned me in his arms. He was still breathing heavily but he managed to speak.

"Unfortunately," Father Sal said, "the Social Security system here in America has always been flawed; never has it been properly calibrated to keep up with the cost of living increases." I was pleasantly exhausted and already dozing off.

"Lover," I told him, "let's just give this a break, I need my beauty rest."

"Why, Bella," he told me, "You do not need the beauty rest. You are beautiful already," and he hugged me close as we drifted off to sleep.

I was dreaming that Sal and I were at the beach at Coney Island, stretched out on a big blanket. The smell of Coppertone was heavy in the air. On a nearby blanket, a radio serenaded us.

He was wearing the kind of old-fashioned, baggy, navy blue knit bathing trunks my grandfather used to wear. I was wearing the flesh-colored bikini that I shoplifted from Bergdorf Goodman's last week. Father Sal liked my bikini very much. I didn't tell him how I got it. My head was on his lap and he was feeding me ripe summer cherries out of a brown paper bag. From my horizontal position I had a lovely view of the calm ocean and the clear blue sky above, unmarked by a single cloud. A crop duster airplane flew into my line of vision, trailing a long white banner. *THIS IS THE END OF THE WORLD AS WE KNOW IT,* the banner said in black block letters.

Why this frightening message? I wanted to point it out to my darling, but before I could, the sky darkened. There was a great clap of thunder and then another and then another. I saw a giant wave rise up out of the ocean and head right for us. I could no longer feel Sal's warm lap beneath me. I woke up. I put my hand out to touch him but he was not there. I was all alone in my empty bed. *He must be in the bathroom*, I thought, *he wouldn't just get up and leave*. Then I heard a faint sound, a whispering. I raised my head higher and saw Sal kneeling at the foot of the bed. He was clutching the big silver cross he always wore around his neck in his hands and rocking back and forth on his knees, his lips moving. I put my head back on the pillow and shut my eyes, pretended I was still sleeping. I could just make out what he was saying.

"Mea culpa, mea culpa, mea maxima culpa," he kept repeating over and over. I knew enough Latin to know this meant he was ashamed.

I wanted to call out to him, tell him there was nothing to be ashamed about, we were so lucky to be in bed together, but then I said nothing. I did not think he would want my company in his dark night of the soul. After a while, he stopped whispering, got back into bed, and pulled the top sheet up to cover us. Then he turned on his side and curled away from me like a question mark.

In a few minutes, he was snoring, but I couldn't fall back to sleep. I wondered how long my amorous padre had been plagued by guilt, whether he had been harboring it since the start of our affair or had just started to feel guilty because was he was falling in love with me, too. Perhaps it was a part of all his romantic adventures; after all, he had told me this was not his first affair, and he was the one who pursued me.

Perhaps feeling guilty turns Sal on, I thought, but I couldn't fall back to sleep. I wondered if he ever wanted to put that cross inside me, to fuck me with it. I lay awake beside him as night opened into morning.

Sal always woke up automatically at five a.m. so he could make it back to his parish for the six o'clock morning mass. I kept my eyes shut as he gently kissed my shoulder, then he dressed and left.

Finally, I slept. When I woke up it was midday, and the room was filled with bright sunlight. I felt groggy and miserable, so I decided to go out to Coney Island to try to leach my unhappiness out in the salt water. On the F train, I was surrounded by noisy families, children drumming their plastic pails, teen lovers with pierced lips and eyebrows, old couples with canes and hearing aids. I seemed to be the only one alone. I wondered if this was my destiny, to be a solitary woman traveling to the beach looking for release from her sorrows, her backpack stuffed with a couple of towels, a big tube of sunblock #45, and the book review section from last week's Sunday *Times*.

Out on the beach, it was a beautiful day, not a cloud in the sky. I put my big towel down next to two old women speaking Russian, sitting on a faux leopard-skin blanket. They were still so glamorous. Their faces were radiant, filled with life, as they laughed and chatted with each other, smoking cigarettes. They were beautifully made up, their lips painted with come-hither reds, their eyebrows tastefully penciled in. Both ladies were wearing black string bikinis, flesh spilling out generously on all sides. They were obviously so happy in their bodies. They agreed to watch my blanket when I went into the water. "Go darling, swim," they chorused.

The ocean was warm and calm as a lake. I turned on my back and floated in the salty brine. After a while, I decided that anything was possible. Maybe I was forbidden fruit to Father Sal, but nothing was forbidden to me. If we split up, I would keep floating on. *As I float into old age,* I promised myself, *I will try to stay as glamorous as the two ladies watching my towel.*

I spent the rest of the afternoon going in and out of the water. The sky remained a clear blue; no planes passed overhead trailing ominous messages. Whatever happened with me and Sal, there would always be the ocean. I felt glad I lived in Brooklyn where the beach is just a subway ride away. I bid good-bye to the ladies. I had learned their names were Anya and Maryasha. Feeling much calmer, I brought a kasha knish at Mrs. Stall's Knishes that I thoroughly savored, eating it slowly on the subway ride home.

I got back to my place with a lot of sand stuck in my jam jar and up in my ass crack. I was eager to get into the shower. However, the red light on my answering machine was blinking merrily and I could not resist hitting the message playback button.

Sal's rich baritone floated out into the room. "My angel," he said, "I was tempted to wake you before I left to kiss your sweet lips but I managed to resist. I had once again a very good time last night. I look forward to Thursday. I will call you again before."

He certainly didn't sound guilty. Hearing his voice made me want him again. Maybe I was making too much of the little scene at the foot of my bed, maybe he was guilty about something else; maybe he used money from the confession box to play the ponies. I stripped and climbed into the shower.

Sal called me Wednesday to confirm our date the next night. We spoke briefly; now he sounded harried, his tone brusque. Could our affair be entering a roller-coaster phase, up and down, up and down like the Cyclone roller coaster at Coney Island?

When I answered the door the next evening, Father Sal was holding not one but two bunches of red roses. He had dark circles under his eyes and he was wearing his priest's shirt with the high collar, and black trousers. He had never showed up for one of our dates dressed all in black before, so it seemed an ominous sign.

"Is this a special occasion?" I asked. He didn't say anything. Upstairs, in my apartment, I took the roses from him and stood on my toes to kiss him. He turned his head so I got his cheek, not his mouth.

"So, you have some whiskey?" he asked. "Let us have a drink."

"Sure," I said, "sit down." I got a couple of glasses and the bottle of Chivas I had bought us a couple of weeks ago because we deserved the best, and brought them to the table. I sat down opposite him and poured us each a stiff one.

"Now," I said, "what about this special occasion?"

He took a big gulp of his drink, swallowed. "Bella," he began, "I do not wish to hurt you, but I cannot continue our arrangement." He looked down at his big hands, more the hands of a mason or bricklayer than a priest. "I think about you too much," he went on. "I'm hearing a confession and I think about your bust. I'm passing among my congregation putting the communion wafer on a congregant's tongue and I think about your tongue on my…and I am filled with impure thoughts."

"I thought you understood that impure is a relative term," I cut in sharply. I knew I should try to be Zen about this, but I do not have a Zen nature. "Didn't you tell me you had made your peace with your wanton nature? Maybe if you are so conflicted about your vocation," I told him, "you should leave the priesthood."

"Never, never," he cried. "It has been my calling since I was a boy, always it was my dream."

He was almost weeping. "I don't know what you want me to say," I told Father Sal. "Do you want me to absolve you, to give you a penance—a hundred Hail Marys—so that after that we can go at it again? Isn't that how it works? The priest absolves the thief and then after the penance, the thief goes out and steals again?"

"You are so sarcastic," he said. "Where is my sweet Bella?"

I finished my drink in a gulp. "She went to the beach," I almost yelled at him. "If you're trying to tell me you want to break it off, okay by me. I don't want to be with someone who feels guilty about making love with me."

His face was all sorrowful, his big eyes liquid with tears. I felt a great sadness filling me, puffing me up like a balloon. I floated up out of my body and looked down on us from the ceiling of my room. I saw an aging sex kitten with a fair figure, whose bottle-blonde hair, dark at the roots, badly needed a touch-up. I saw a portly priest with a big bald spot on the top of his head and a huge erection clearly visible beneath the fabric of his black trousers. I saw two middle-aged people who had already licked their little plate of happiness clean. I decided to try not to make this awkward scene even worse.

I returned to my body as Sal was finishing off his scotch. "Well, we had some good times, didn't we?" I managed to say, in a dismal effort to be a good sport. He smiled a tight little smile.

I gulped down my scotch; it burned like hellfire in my throat. Then, I couldn't help myself; I put my hand out to rest on his very visible knob. I gave it a few solid yanks.

"How about just one more for the road?" I said. I knew he could not resist me.

I moved my chair closer to his, put my knee between his sturdy thighs. I kept a firm grip on him as I pulled and squeezed, pulled and squeezed. "Ah, Bella, Bella," he sighed unzipping his fly, "but I did not bring, I do not have a...a..." I knew he was searching for the word *condom*.

"But I have one," I said, and quicker then you could say *the wages of sin are death*, I sprang up, went into my bedroom, and got a condom out of my condom box.

I had it out of the foil packet by the time I got back into the kitchen. He was holding his rod between his hands. I wondered if he was praying to it.

I bent over and pulled the condom on him. I kissed his lips, dipping my tongue into the sweet cistern of his mouth. I spread my legs and climbed astride him, taking all of him deep into me. My thick cunt hair must have tickled him as I slid up and down, down and up, because he giggled a little. I kept on faster and faster until the friction generated between us was so great, I thought we would burst into flame. I opened my eyes to see his eyes screwed shut and his face all covered with sweat. My whole body was wet as if all the love juice inside me was seeping out from my pores. From where we were joined, I smelled ashes and peanuts and bitter red wine.

He arched his back abruptly and just when I was ready too, shot his loving spirit deep into my heart.

Weightless and free, we bobbed up and down like a top floating in the ocean at Coney Island, but only for a few moments did we enjoy this tender release.

Then he stirred beneath me, his silver cross pressed into my chest between my breasts. I could feel it, even through the fabric of my dress, cutting into me, branding me.

I climbed off. He sighed, he seemed to be weeping. I peeled the condom from his cock and put it into the garbage can next to the refrigerator. I didn't offer him another drink.

"Are you all right?" he asked.

"Sure," I answered. "Great."

"Oh, my Bella," he began.

"Please," I said. "Don't get all sentimental, just go."

He stood up and tucked his now shy scepter back inside his pants and zipped up. He looked sadly around my cluttered kitchen. "Bella, Bella," he said, "I will never forget you." He took a step toward me, his arms out as if to embrace me.

"You better go," I told him, "before you get tempted again," and I turned my back to him. I heard him take the few steps to the door and I heard when it shut behind him. Then I heard his footsteps growing fainter as he walked down the hall. I couldn't help but wonder if this was really the end.

MIKE KIMERA

Have a Nice Day

I SEND YOU THIS MESSAGE on the beeper: *Open the box in private—but open it at once.*

Five minutes later, at 11:30, UPS delivers a parcel marked PERSONAL to your desk at work. Everyone notices as you go to the bathroom immediately with the parcel.

The package contains: a note, a condom, and a large black dildo; one of those anatomically correct but way-out-of-scale dildos, all veins and ridges, made out of silicone so that they bend and feel warm to the touch. The toy looks huge in your hand. You find yourself playing with it; feeling the weight in the palm of your hand. Without thinking, you rub the head against your cheek. Then you remember the note. It says, *Take off your panties. Fold them and put them in your purse. Slide the condom over the dildo and push the dildo all the way into your cunt. DO NOT fuck yourself with it. Go to our table at Starbucks at 12:15.*

Your cunt is very wet.

Surely, you think, *this huge dildo will never fit.*

Then you realize you will have to go back into the office with the beast inside you and wait until it's time to walk to the coffee shop round the corner. You think of how this monster will feel in your cunt as you walk. You notice that you are squeezing the rubber cock in your hand. With sudden determination, you take off your panties—red silk today—fold them and put them in your purse.

You have just ripped the foil on the condom when you hear people enter the toilet. You don't have time to wait. You roll the condom down over the black cock in your hands—this feels so real you half expect it to spit come at you—hoping no one will recognize that condom smell. You put one foot up on the toilet bowl, open yourself as wide as you can, and start to push the toy in.

Someone enters the stall next to yours. You are struggling to take all of the dildo inside you. Trying not to be heard. Trying not to just fuck yourself crazy with this invader. You get most of it inside you. Two inches protrude. You sit on the toilet seat and, balancing on the tip of the dildo, you push hard. The remainder slides in slowly, making you groan.

The black dildo is now deep in your cunt. You pull down your skirt and step out of the cubicle. In the mirror, you see that your nipples are very prominent and that your legs are slightly parted causing your skirt to rise up a little. People are bound to notice something in the office.

You return to your desk. The beeper goes. You read *How does it feel?*

The beeper goes again. *Cross your legs.*

You obey and feel the rubber cock move inside you. Three minutes 'till you leave for Starbucks. A colleague comes to your desk and asks if you'd like to go to lunch. You think he's looking at your hard nipples. Can he smell you? You want to look at his cock to see if it's hard, but you daren't. You smile and decline his offer.

Walking has never been so difficult. Although you know how tightly held the cock is, you still worry the thing will slip out. You feel as though your legs are spread wide as you walk. Your hips sway slightly more than normal. This attracts attention. You try to hurry and have to stand still suddenly. The pressure is too much. You walk slowly to our table at Starbucks. The beeper goes: *Don't turn around. I'm watching you. Fits snugly, doesn't it?* You reach Starbucks as you finish reading the message.

Our table is taken. A beautiful black woman in a stylish business suit of a bright yellow is sitting at one of the chairs. You turn to look for me when the woman smiles, stands, and embraces you.

"Jenny," she says, hugging you to her. She is six feet tall, slim, with long black hair, a wide mouth, bright teeth, high cheekbones. There is no blouse under the business jacket.

As she hugs you she whispers, "It's a very BIG dildo, isn't it, Jenny? Sit very close to me, raise your skirt so your bare ass is on the chair, and keep your legs a little apart. Your man sent me." She kisses you on both cheeks and sits down. You are shocked. I've never done this to you before.

Your beeper goes *DO AS SHE SAYS.* When you look up, you see that her eyes are focused on your nipples. Seeing your look, she smiles and licks her lips. You sit. The shiny aluminum chair is cold against your flesh. She moves her chair closer to yours and, as she passes you a latte with her left hand, her right hand slides up your thigh to your cunt.

"Don't spill the coffee on this nice skirt," she says and looks you in the eyes as her fingers trace your swollen cunt lips and feel the butt of the dildo at the entrance to your pussy. You sit absolutely still.

She pushes gently on the dildo but it doesn't move. Her fingers stroke back down your thigh in slow circles. She brings her fingers to her lips and licks them. "I love a tight wet cunt," she says. "I was told you would be good." You look down at your coffee. "Nice nipples, too. Glad to see there's no bra...I'm going to use you, Jenny—with your permission—I *do* have your permission, don't I?" she pauses.

You look up. "Yes, you have my permission to use me...I would like that."

She makes a call on her cell phone and a white stretch limo pulls up. She leads you to the limo by the hand. You worry about getting in without flashing your dildo-filled cunt at the world. People know you here. She solves the problem for you. Once the door is open, she pushes you hard on the back of the head and you fall into the limo face-first, ass in the air. As you scramble for balance you hear the sound of yourself coming. The video in the limo shows you being fucked by me and coming hard.

"Don't just lie there, Jenny, take a seat and watch the show—I've seen it twice. By the way, my name's Lily." You look up and then past her and finally you see me sitting in the center of a bench seat. I look at you but say nothing.

Lily lifts you easily and places you in the center of the bench seat opposite. She ties each of your ankles to a car door, spreading your legs so wide the muscles on the inside of your thighs tremble. Lily pushes back your skirt so that your whole ass is visible. She lifts both of your hands above your head and ties them to a headrest. Your back is arched. Only your ass is on the seat. You sway slightly as the car moves.

Lily sits beside me and we both watch you. The video is on loop and starts with you on the floor, tied, with my cock in your mouth. Lily kisses me, unzips my pants, and frees my cock. I push her head down on it while keeping my eyes on you. The black dildo is visible in your swollen cunt. Already, I can smell your juices. Your eyes plead with me for attention.

I pull Lily's head off my cock and push her toward you. "You're getting the seat damp, Jenny," Lily says. Her fingers trace the outline of your wet cunt lips around the dildo. You moan and look away. She kneels between your legs and licks your clit. Your ass bounces on the seat.

"Show her," I say.

Lily takes off the yellow jacket. Her breasts are very round. They both have large gold nipple rings. She hefts one breast in her hand and licks the nipple with her long tongue. Shimmying out of the skirt, she exposes a shaved pussy and a tight muscled ass. She is wearing a harness around her hips and between her legs. Seeing you look at it, she points to a ring on the harness just above her clit. "This is what the butt of that dildo slots into, Jenny. I'm going to have such fun fucking you with it. Maybe we should see how well it fits your ass."

You look at Lily, licking your lips. "Come fuck me with your big cock, bitch," you moan, your hips swaying and your pussy gripping the dildo.

I grin at your response. "I told you she was good, Lily, enjoy her."

Lily licks her way up your thighs. Her tongue penetrates your ass. She pushes deeply into you. Her strong tongue passes through your rosebud. She sucks hard. Her large lips move up. She takes the dildo in her teeth and pulls it back by an inch. She slots it into the belt.

"Fuck me," you say and push yourself forward, pressing the dildo against her mound. You feel the huge dildo slide deep in you as Lily rams it in and out of you. Bouncing your hips off the car seat to meet each thrust, you push back on the dildo so she feels it against her clit. Both of you moan as she fucks you.

I reach over and pull on her nipple rings as I tweak your tit. I push two fingers up your ass as Lily pushes hard, burying the dildo deep in your cunt. You pull on the ropes as you feel the dildo stretch your tight pussy, then push back on it, making Lily moan. Faster and faster she fucks into you, your body squirming as I ram my fingers up your hot ass. Lily pushes deep into you, grinding her hips against you as she comes. I shove my fingers further into your ass and pinch your clit, making you scream as you come.

I release your hands and legs, sit on the seat you have made damp and then retie your hands behind your back, leaving your legs free as you kneel in front of me. Grabbing your head, I force my cock into your wet mouth. You feel Lily's hands stroking your back as your lips slide up and down my hard cock. I push your head down onto my cock. It lodges with comfortable familiarity deep in your throat.

A shiver runs through your body as you groan against my cock; Lily pushes her fingers into your ass. Looking into my eyes, you suck me hard and deep, with your tongue twirling around my cock. Lily fingers your ass as I fuck my cock in and out of your mouth. I hear you moan and feel you jerk as Lily pushes the big dildo up your tight ass. I watch the big black dildo disappear, spreading your asshole as inch by inch it sinks into your tight tunnel. Your ass squirms prettily as Lily impales you on the huge rod. Reflexively, your ass ring tightens, fighting to keep out the dildo that's splitting you.

I keep your mouth on my cock as you arch your back trying to lift your head up and scream. Lily grins at me as she twists the dildo in your ass making your body jerk. I watch as she pulls it out until just the crown is surrounded by your ass ring. I nod my head at her and with one forceful stroke she buries the dildo deep into your ass as I push down on your head and flex my hips, forcing my cock fully into your throat. You feel my cock pulse as I come down your throat. "Drink it," I say, and feel your throat tighten as you swallow.

I untie your hands and hug you to me. Lily has detached the dildo from her harness leaving it buried in your ass.

"Help me tie Lily," I say. Lily lies back in the seat, taking up more of it than you did. We spread her legs so wide the pink inside her slit is visible. With clever knots you tie her outstretched legs to the bench opposite, making her lean forward slightly. You kneel back to look at her.

I raise your hands above your head and slip off your top. It is the first time Lily has seen your breasts. From behind you I cup them, kissing your neck, working on the hard nipples, while you smile at Lily. The elegant gold nipple clamps close brutally over each of your nipples in turn. You bite your lip as I connect each of your clamps to one of Lily's nipple rings by five inches of gold chain. You are very close to one another now but not touching.

I pull you backward on your heels and then further, until your breasts and hers are both stretched and the little gold chains are taut. Lily's eyes go wide and I realize she is a screamer. I reach into your purse and find the panties you placed there earlier. "Use these to gag her," I say and let go of you.

You climb between Lily's legs and place the gusset of your panties against her tongue, filling her mouth with them. Then you kiss her throat, hands resting on her breasts.

"Lily likes to be fisted," I say "but she's never been fisted in her little brown hole. I think you could put one of your small hands in each hole at the same time, don't you, Jenny?" Lily's starts to struggle, shaking her head and jiggling the chains that bind you together.

You make eye contact with her, smile wickedly and say, "I would enjoy that." You kiss Lily on her lips and whisper in her ear, "I do have your permission to use you don't I, Lily? To use you harder than you've ever been used before?" Lily pauses, feeling your tongue trace its way down her neck. She nods briefly but will not look at you.

I smear K-Y over your hands and wrists. You slowly work your fingers into her rear hole, one at a time, until you can get your entire hand inside of her. Lily thrashes as you slide into her past your wrist. You pull back a little, then you thrust your hand all the way in. You place your left hand on her cunt. The lips are swollen. Pink is clearly visible. Juices are running from her cunt to where your arm is buried in her ass. You laugh and slide you hand easily into her pussy.

I watch your delight as you discover that you can rub your hands together. Even muffled by the gag, Lily's screams are loud. I turn on the stereo. The lyrics "I wanna lover with a slow hand" drown out Lily's moans. My cock is hard again. I slip it into your cunt from behind, feeling how the dildo in your ass squeezes me. You fuck Lily to the rhythm of my cock in your cunt. Lily's body is now covered in sweat.

I know I won't last long inside you. Your whole cunt is massaging my cock. On the outward pull of your arms, you lean back so you can pull Lily's breasts with your own. On the inward stroke you push deep into her and lean your breasts against her. With each stroke your cunt massages my cock. You are close to orgasm now. My hand finds your bud and coaxes it. As you come, you push deeper yet into Lily and lie gasping against her breasts. She hardly notices; she is coming in both holes at once, trapping your hands in her flesh. I come hard, watching her, watching you.

"Time to go back to work, Jenny."

You look at me confused. I kiss your forehead and pull your hands from Lily. I hand you Wet Ones to clean yourself with.

You reach to remove the dildo from your ass. "Leave it there. I'll beep you to say when you can remove it." I take your panties from Lily's mouth. "Put these on and straighten your skirt," I say as I gently remove the nipple clamps.

"You have done well, Jenny, I'm pleased with you." The limo halts as you slide the top back on over your sensitive nipples. I step out of the car and pull you to your feet on the curb.

"You'll want to freshen up," I say and you become aware of your smudged lipstick and disheveled hair. You are outside the main entrance to your office.

I kiss your forehead, whisper, "Have a nice day" in your ear, get into the limo and leave.

SOMMER MARSDEN

A GENUINE MOTHERFUCKER

I NEVER EVER FUCK THEM until I know their triggers. This can require patience beyond measure. Some give them up the first night. Some make me dig like an archaeologist searching for a tiny treasure. Tom fell in between.

It was our third date and we had just had a lovely meal. I had the fish. He had the steak. I opened up a new vein of conversation, sipping my rum and coke. Still searching for my treasure. Employing that patience I needed.

"Are you an only child?" I really didn't care, but sometimes you have to fly blind.

He nodded and polished off his Rolling Rock. "Raised by a single mother." He beamed when he spoke the sentence. My internal radar emitted a little vibration. Flying blind can pay off at times.

"What about your dad?"

His big open face clouded over. His skin paled a little. A frown tugged at the corners of his usually jovial mouth. "Left when I was four. Fucker," he muttered the last part but the hatred in that one word was like a bright spark in a dark room.

"So you and your mom are close?" I asked, watching. I studied him casually but I was waiting. If I had struck gold, I would know right away.

His face flushed with a look of adoration. "We are. She was my best friend growing up. She did everything for me. Sacrificed so much. My mother is a saint. And beautiful," he sighed and his eyes glazed over just a little.

Bingo. I wanted to laugh and clap my hands. I had done it. What I had here was a genuine motherfucker. At least in his heart. Hated his father, adored his mother. Big old, lumbering, happy-go-lucky Tommy wanted to fuck his mommy.

I could do that.

"You know," I whispered, leaning in close so he could see down the bodice of my dress, take in the cleavage that had been dusted with powder that sparkled and smelled like vanilla, "Why don't you invite me home, Tom? For a nightcap. I'll follow you home. Okay?"

He threw his shoulders back and a grin lit his face, all thoughts of mommy gone from his mind—for now. "I thought you'd never ask, Nina."

He didn't even get his front door locked before he was on me. He rubbed his hard-on against the seam of my ass through the thin fabric of my dress. "God, you're beautiful."

He nuzzled the back of my neck and a pleasant tingling sensation shot up under my hair, invaded my scalp. I shivered just a little and laughed. “Why don’t you get naked and fuck me?

His seduction stuttered just a little at my blunt statement. Then the grin was back and the tie was off and he followed me to his bedroom like a trained pony. I assumed it was his when I entered since he lived alone. I shucked the dress and flipped off my heels. I left the garter belt and hose on, though. Somehow I thought they might come in handy. A nostalgic reminder.

I was right. I caught him staring. Following the smoky black hose from my ankles to mid thigh. Tracking the trail of the elastic band that held them up with that glazed gaze. He practically consumed the garter belt with his eyes.

“Like what you see?” I asked and let my legs fall open just a touch. The satin thong I wore was soaked. A stain of wetness, just a touch darker than the black of the thong.

Tom bounded onto the bed like an overgrown dog and I laughed just a little as I bounced sideways. In a lot of ways, he really was nothing more than an enormous child.

“Ooooh, Nina, I want you so bad.”

Even this sounded childish and I had to press my lips together to keep myself from snickering.

He barreled on as he ran a hand up my leg. The nylon emitted a sibilant whisper as if it were happy. Happy being fondled by his huge hand. The calluses on his palms caught on the sheer barrier every few inches. “I want to make you come. I want to make you come and then come again,” he sighed. Like a child rattling off his wish list for

Santa. "I want to see you come and feel you come and taste you come."

I smiled at Tom. I wanted this, too. However, my real payoff would come later. When I was home. Just me and my memories. But I nodded and gave him a motherly smile.

I let him tell me all that he wanted to do to me. I let him build his confidence and his hopes. And I smiled the whole time.

His cock was big like the rest of him. Tall, broad shoulders, big hands, big feet, big dick. It was nearly violet, straining with anticipation. Bouncing and seeking the heat of my cunt blindly, as if it had a mind of its own. If I hadn't been so turned on by finding his trigger, by what was about to happen, I would have been fascinated with that prick of his. As it stood, I simply reached out and stroked it with my long fingers, smoothing my thumb over the tiny slit, spreading the first tiny jewel of fluid so that he jumped in my hand, let out a moan of pleasure. I almost laughed. This would be easy. Almost too easy. But I would take it. I had been waiting what felt like years to break Tom.

I tugged his cock with one hand, and his eyes went hooded and darker in the blink of an eye. I guided him toward me, the waiting wetness between my legs.

"You're really wet," he muttered. He sounded drunk with lust and need and want. The headiest cocktail of all. He forced two thick fingers into my cunt and sighed so loudly it was as if he had buried his cock deep inside of me.

Those long plump fingers worked me sweetly from the inside, but I was growing impatient so I tugged his erection a little harder. And he came forward willingly. He slid the thick length into me in one agonizingly slow thrust. I repressed the urge to shove myself up against him and bury him as far as he would go.

"Oh," I sighed in his ear. A nice old-fashioned sex sound. *Oh. Oh, my. How big you are down there....*

He stiffened just a little at that murmured word. I smiled but he couldn't see me. My lips were nestled behind his ear. His body told the tale, though.

Tom moved in me gracefully. Surprisingly so for such a big man. There wasn't a smidge of awkwardness as he fucked me. Each thrust perfect, hitting all the swollen spots that needed to be tended to. He held himself over me and when he angled his face down to kiss me, I parted my lips for him and sucked his tongue greedily. His features were starker, more angular and I knew it was right. He had reached the point where it didn't just feel *good*, the pleasure had grown swollen. The need was strong.

So, I did what I do so well.

I watched his face and started to whisper, "Fuck Mommy real good, Tommy. Mommy likes your big, hard cock in her pussy. Tommy, Tommy...such a good boy."

His face tensed for a moment and a look of panic swept across it like the shadow of a storm cloud. But he didn't stop moving. Wouldn't stop moving. His cock shoved higher and harder, his breathing sounded like a freight train.

"I'll let you eat me when you're done. You'll have to clean your plate, though. Get it all."

He stiffened against me, growing rigid and tense. He was trying. Trying so hard I almost felt bad for him. Trying to hold off the orgasm.

Trying to ignore the triggers. My knowledge of his filthy little secret. My giving him this dark little gift.

"I'll let you eat Mommy real good, Tommy. Eat me all up," I hissed in his ear and tightened my cunt around his pumping cock.

On a groaned "Ah, fuck" he came.

I took it all in. Absorbed it. Snorted it. Ate it. Each flicker of humiliation. Each wince and each shade of shame that crossed his face. I didn't come. He knew it and was ashamed. What he didn't know was that I did it on purpose. He gave me all I need to get off and he hadn't a clue.

Men think of it as premature ejaculation. Failure. To me it is blind, naked need. Stark and beautiful and the most enticing drug on earth. To see a man snap. To see his shame. To hear him promise and preach and talk about what he will give me. Then I push him over the edge and watch how it happens. How the need can eat the owner if the owner isn't careful.

And he did eat me, partially as penance I believe. To alleviate some of his shame. Some of his embarrassment. He ate my pussy as if to say he was sorry. He wasn't bad at all and I offered him an orgasm to help him not feel so bad. It was good, but it wasn't what I was after. I gave him the orgasm out of pity.

I left him with a kiss and a pat on the arm and I nearly ran to my car. I drove as fast as I could without getting pulled over, my cunt achy and twitchy. Contracting and flickering in my thong. Reminding me that the night was not over for me.

In the house, I flopped on the bed, shoved my thong to the side and shoved three fingers into my body. My eyes tightly closed, my breathing a rasping sound in my own ears, I flicked my clit and the resounding echo of sheer pleasure I received told me it wouldn't take long.

Behind my closed lids, I saw him clearly. I heard the delicious phantom, "Ah, fuck" in my ears. I could see the pain, the shame, the humiliation. I could see the moment when his control snapped and so did mine. My cunt seized around my working fingers, fluid sliding down to coat my hand as I came like a summer storm. Long and loud and fierce. His humiliated face frozen in time in my mind.

MATHILDE MADDEN

THE THINGS YOU DO WHEN YOU'RE IN LOVE

I LOVE THE WAY WE DO THINGS differently from other people.

Like, when you come home from work, you don't just take off your coat, you take off all your clothes and hang them up in the hallway. Everything except your collar. Which isn't a collar like a dog would wear but a silver chain, so you can wear it at work and no one will think there is anything weird about it. Except that it is too small for you to take off without opening the fastening. And the fastening is a lock, and you don't have the key.

But we do a lot of stuff the same as other people too. I like to cook and you wash up. I take out the rubbish because you're naked. I like you being naked more than I don't like taking out the rubbish. We watch TV and I always hold the remote control. Then we go to bed.

But when we eat you sometimes don't sit at the table. You sometimes kneel on the floor and eat out of a dog bowl. You choose. You always set the table while I'm cooking and you choose where you put your place and what kind of flatware you're having.

Some days, when you choose the dog bowl, I just roll my eyes at you, like, *My boyfriend is such a huge pervert*, and some days when I see you've chosen to eat out of a dog bowl on the floor at my feet I just want to jump you. And some days I *do* jump you.

When we go to bed, we'll most often lie next to each other in the dark and masturbate. Again, that's a bit different from most people, I know, but that's what we like to do.

I say stuff to you like, "I want to gag you."

And you say, "Okay," or, "I'd really like that," or sometimes, "Thank you."

And then sometimes I get an actual gag out and you wear it while you jerk yourself off next to me or sometimes we just talk about it and I say stuff like, "Can I gag you? Would you like that?"

And you say, "Sure."

"Say it."

"I'd like it if you gagged me."

"Why would you like it? No, first, I'll tell you why *I'd* like it. I like the way you look when you have a gag in your mouth. You have this sort of helpless expression that just does it for me." I pause. "And there's the other thing too."

"I know. Humiliating me."

"Yeah. And I really like that you said it. Now tell me why you'd like it."

You don't speak for a moment. Your hands keep moving and so do mine in the quiet. Then you say, "I like it that you force something into my mouth and I can't get it out. It makes me feel owned and violated."

It's funny, after you say that thing about being violated I can't stop thinking about more ways to violate you. And suddenly, every time I look at you all I can think about is raping you.

So I tell you. I say, "I want to rape you."

You turn around. You're in the middle of the washing up. You're naked apart from your collar and a pair of rubber gloves. I've seen you like this before. Every evening since you moved in. I don't know why it's funnier now. Maybe because I've just told you I want to rape you.

You say, "So what do you want? You want me to fake it? Struggle? Try and run? Beg you not to? Get overpowered? Scream for help?"

My nose itches. I'm rubbing it when I say, "Yeah, maybe. I don't know really. I just want you to be getting raped."

"Okay," you say, turning back around to face the sink.

"Is that 'okay' like a consent? Okay to being raped?"

"Sure."

That night, I tie you to the bed and just before I climb onto your very hard erection, I tell you that you're not going to come tonight. You groan and squirm like you can't tell if it's a good thing or a bad thing. And, God, that's hot.

You say, "When, then?"

"I don't know. I haven't decided."

"It's really difficult when I don't know how long."

"You know," I say as I move up and down, "I've seen some guys on the Web who've gone a year. A whole year locked up in one of those devices. Haven't we got one of those for you somewhere? You don't want me to start thinking about something like that for you? Could you manage that?"

Underneath me you laugh. "*You'd* never manage it. You love it when I come."

"Well, whatever, I don't want you to come for a few days because I want you to come when you get raped." I think about you scared and struggling. I think about you trying to cry out and having your mouth covered by a big hand. It isn't my hand.

Three days and you haven't come. And it's been the weekend so you have been mostly naked. And you've got to the point where you're hard most of the time.

You're getting kind of grumpy. You're asking for it.

"Are you going to rape me today? Jump me and I'll struggle and fight you. Tie me down. I'll beg and, just, whatever."

You stand up and start to clear away the breakfast things. Your cock is really hard and tight against your flat belly. You know, you really are very, very good looking.

It's been three whole meals since you ate from your bowl on the floor. A sure sign you're sulking. I get up and follow you into the kitchen.

You're running water into the sink. Pulling on your rubber gloves. I come up behind you and put my arms around your chest. You sigh. I really do love it when you're frustrated.

I just hold you. You keep washing up.

You say, "You're just going to stand there, aren't you? You're not going to do anything. I know you aren't, but I really like to have it confirmed."

"I want you to be desperate."

"I am, baby."

"I want you so desperate that you'd agree to anything. Consent to anything."

"I am. You know I am. Whatever you want, you know that." You're still washing up, dipping the breakfast bowls into the sudsy water.

I move my hands down your body to your taut stomach. Sometimes I play this game with myself where I try and decide which part of your body I like the best. What? Do I objectify you too much? Anyway, I can never decide, but your stomach often makes the top five.

So does your cock. And, right now, even though I'm not touching it I can feel the air move as your erection twitches. God, I love you. I say, "Yeah. I know. I don't know. I want you to consent to things that you wouldn't otherwise. I don't know. Is that weird?"

You turn around in my arms. You're naked and you're collared and you put your wet rubber-gloved hands on my shoulders. You're smiling and your erection presses into my belly. "Consent's always weird. If you've got a plan, baby, well, you've never let me down before."

I look down at the place where your cock is sandwiched between us. "And you don't mind? I mean, you don't mind having to wait?"

"Oh, I *mind*. I can't concentrate on anything and I've got to go to work like this. It's killing me. And it's so fucking hot, baby."

You kiss me. You taste like Weetabix.

There's this place I know.

It's a garage. A filling station. In the middle of nowhere. So I say we should get in the car and drive there and fill up the car with gas.

It's not the nearest place to get gas. We still have half a tank. That's not why we're going.

You pull up. You fill up. After you've paid, I tell you I want to use the lavatory. I tell you I want you to come too. I tell you to move the car and park it where it isn't blocking the gas pumps.

In my handbag I have the following things: handcuffs and some nipple clamps and a lipstick. I'm going to hurt you. The lipstick is the only thing I added specially. I always carry the other things.

The lavatory at this semideserted filling station in the middle of nowhere is disgusting. Dirty and sordid. I've told you before how much I'd like to see you naked in here. In this dank little room lit by a bare bulb with an ancient toilet that has one of those high level tanks and a filthy broken sink.

You probably remember me saying that. Because you strip, without being asked, as soon as the door is closed. Your cock is hard and you're a fucking pervert and you're probably thinking that this is the place where you're going to get raped. You're thinking right.

But I kiss you first. The walls aren't tiled, just painted. I push your naked back up against one of them as we kiss. It's freezing cold and filthy dirty. You're panting and so needy-desperate for this and that's making me hotter than anything. Naked and hard in this filthy place, you own me. Nobody's really playing slave boy games tonight because neither of us is really free.

God, I love you naked. I love your body. I kiss you and touch you. It's nice.

"You need to get on your knees now."

I guide you a little and you kneel down facing the toilet. I put the lid down so you can rest on it and pull your arms out in front of you and cuff you, twisting the chain around the pipe that runs down from the high tank.

Then I take out the clamps and lean over your back so my breasts and my belly push against you and I reach around and snap each clamp onto one of your nipples, which are already really fucking hard.

You yelp.

I rub the little pinch of flesh that is trapped in each clamp and I put my mouth close to your ear and call you some demeaning names. I keep doing this, calling you dirty and hard and wet, to get you through, while I attach the chains from the clamps to the pipe with a little piece of twine. Everything is pulled tight. And you're hard. And it hurts.

You're breathing heavily and so am I. Your cock is leaking. I look at you on your knees on the floor. The floor is filthy. Covered in grime. I want you so much. It's making me nuts. Look at me. No sane person would want to be here. In this vile place in the middle of the night. It's cold. Cold. And the coldest thing of all is this sudden feeling deep in my stomach. A frozen ache.

I get that sudden, certain rush of what-the-fuck-are-you-doing?

"This is fucked up shit," I say quietly. "This is the only thing I've ever wanted my whole life. I'm scared of myself for wanting this. I'm scary. God, look at what I'm doing. Look at this. Look at me."

And you say, "No. Look at *me*."

Who wouldn't want to look at you? Naked and chained to a toilet. You're helpless. Trapped here with this thing that used to be me. And you're the bravest man I've ever met.

I love you. It makes me strong.

I take my lipstick out of my handbag. And I pull off the cap. Aesthetics are very important. I like the way the greasy lipstick slides across your skin.

That's what I'm thinking about when I hold the lipstick and watch it slide as I write PLEASE RAPE ME on your back. The red is so bright. Crass and cruel and offensive. Like the sentiment.

I turn around. I walk out the door and into the night.

I sit in the car with the heater and the radio blasting. I play with the key in the ignition. Starting the engine. Fooling myself I might drive away. I'm playing mind fuck on myself. How crazy am I?

I can see the door of the lavatory from here. I know no one has gone in there. I'm pretty sure you're okay. Then I see the man.

You're big. And he's not as tall or as built as you, but he's no light-weight either. Older than you. Bald. Not pretty. He's walking across the forecourt towards the lavatory. I swallow. I watch him go in and when he doesn't come out, after thirty seconds or so, I start to masturbate.

I know the man in the lavatory would only be able to do two things when faced with you in the state I left you in. Rape you or come out and get help. When he doesn't come out I'm sure of what he's doing.

I didn't gag you because I wanted him to cover your mouth with his hand to keep you quiet. I think about that. And about the way your invitation to your rapist is being smeared away as he fucks you hard and heartlessly. And about how small and helpless and hopeless and abandoned you must feel. Poor boy. Poor beautiful boy getting fucked.

So sulliable. So wanton. So inevitable that this should happen to you left unattended.

I think about him touching your cock. And think that you might not even need to be touched. You're so on edge right now. So on edge.

I come. He goes.

I fetch you and dress you. I get you out. I do what I need to do and it's a bit messy and a bit stumbly but we get there. It's kind of okay, considering. I put you on the backseat. You're on another planet.

I drive off, out onto the main road, and the car is just purring. I'll probably tell you later who he was. That I knew him. That I told him what to do to you. Maybe you realized when you felt that he knew just how to touch you to make you come especially hard. That he pressed the pad of his thumb against your prostate just right. Maybe you guessed then that I had explained to him what I wanted. That I had been in control of everything. Because details are important to me.

But I'm not going to talk to you about that just yet. You're shifting around on the backseat. There's no other sound but the engine for a little while and then you say, "Baby, I'm really hungry. When we get home, do you want to have some toast?"

Outside in the dark, I watch the lights of the other cars, the street-lights, the cats' eyes. I love you. I'm laughing.

ALANA NOËL VOTH

WAIF

IT'S INEXORABLE BY NOW, how a man drives to a corner where a boy stands like waif cake with bruised eyes like blue frosting and a crumbling smile that fails to hide crooked teeth. Beneath a rare glare of sunshine, the boy's hair looks the color of cinnamon, which the man had sprinkled on his toast this morning while he stared out a window at a river, barges and boats below too far away for detail.

This morning, the man wished he'd missed details. Details at work. Details on corners. Except there'd been no way he wouldn't have recognized the boy the day he drove on his way to hopeless oblivion and then saw the boy instead. A bright echo of a familiar photo. The man had braked alongside the curb, and then the boy had leaned into the passenger-side window. "Want to watch me jerk off?"

You can want something in order to hurt somebody else; you can want something to make yourself feel better; or you can, and this was the tricky one, want something because you want life to turn out better for another person.

The man had nodded, wanting to hurt someone else and make himself feel better.

The boy had opened the car door and gotten in. The man had driven six blocks to an alley: industrial gut encased by brick and steel. The boy had taken his cock out, and the man had watched and bit the inside of his cheek and experienced anger, arousal, regret.

Now, the boy gets in the man's car again, and the man feels surprised by a sense of intimacy. He could almost hug the boy. He sees the boy's freckles like dots he'd connect with a pencil or clues he might find in a financial ledger. The man feels himself shrink away, harden. "You drink?" he asks pulling the car away from the curb.

"Why, we getting me drunk today?"

"No. It's just you never smell like alcohol." The man's former boss had often showed up to work smelling like his cocktail lunch.

"That's a bad thing?"

The man steers the car left. "No, I'm glad."

"Why would it matter to you?"

The man doesn't look at the boy. "Drinking gets you in trouble."

"Not me," the boy says. "Jeez, you sound like my dad."

The man feels sweat on the back of his neck and jerks the car to the left.

The boy falls sideways. "Shit." He sits up. "What's the problem?"

"Nothing." The man grips the steering wheel with both hands.

"Yeah, you should have a drink or ten," the boy says.

"I don't think so." He feels tense.

"Dude, anyone can tell you're stressed."

The man wipes his forehead with his sleeve. Cotton shirt. He hadn't worn a suit in weeks.

"So I was wondering. How old are you? I've never asked."

The man plays the boy's game. "Why would it matter to you? I'm just old, right?"

"Ha, okay. I'll guess. You're...forty...*ish*, right?"

The man doesn't answer.

"Pretty hot for an old guy though."

This brings the man joy, the kind he didn't think he was capable of anymore because it's not mean spirited but pure. The man breathes it in for a moment then changes the subject, doesn't realize he's gone on the defensive because he feels possessive of the boy.

"Why do you stand on a street corner all day?"

"So you can buy me."

The man looks at him. The boy smiles. He doesn't want the boy to stand on a street corner anymore.

"Dude, I'm totally legal."

The boy doesn't understand. But does the man understand any better?

"You have a boyfriend?" the boy asks.

"No."

"Wife?"

"No." The man stares ahead at the road.

The boy chuckles and the sound of it is redemptive maybe. Here he was on the street, and the boy still chuckled.

"Want to watch me jerk off?"

"Yes."

The man looks. The boy pulls down his zipper and yanks his cock out: a cock like dough; the boy works his hand into the bowel of his lap and pulls the soft shaft. The man tries to drive and watch at the same time and is stunned by how much he wants this. Maybe more than he'd wanted to bust his boss. The boy half smiles. His belly reminds the man of a gulley. Maybe for once he should feed him. The man fits a finger into the boy's mouth. The boy sucks the man's finger while he jerks his cock. In the same alley, the man stops the car. The boy has deep-throated his finger. The man's cock is hard.

"Do you fuck boys?" Inside his slacks, the man feels cramped; his erection is cruel and painful. The boy has closed his eyes and looks dreamy. The man pulls his finger from his mouth so he can answer.

"Not exactly. I suck a lot of cock." The boy has spit shining on his lips. He breathes heavy. The man paints the line of the boy's jaw with the spit and feels the boy clench his muscles. Maybe he grinds his teeth when he sleeps and never rests.

"Where do you live now?"

"Places." The boy rubs his cheek against the inside of the man's arm.

"Safe places?"

"Safe as I've ever been." The boy kisses the man's pulse point, the taut chords in his wrist.

The man pulls his arm back. His heart beats too fast. He rolls down his window then turns the ignition so the radio comes on. "What do you like?" He presses buttons.

"Adult contemporary."

"What?"

"Isn't that what you like?"

The man pushes another button, hard with his finger, and brings up a song. The man listens: Glen Campbell, "Rhinestone Cowboy."

"Oh, this sets a mood." The boy laughs. At last, the man laughs too, and the feeling of it isn't so far from screaming his head off or sobbing.

"Hey, want me to suck you off?" The cock in the boy's hand is hard now, huge. He could tear a man open with it, rip something out of him.

The man holds the steering wheel. Glen Campbell sings. He releases the steering wheel and lets his hands fall limp on each side of him. He feels like a monkey, a jerk. Sweat has sealed his asscheeks shut. The car has slid down a gullet of two buildings. The city is impossibly huge, like the boy's cock. The man rolls his head to one side to look at the boy in the seat beside him.

"Come for me."

"Kiss me first."

"I can't kiss you."

"Not good enough for you?"

"No, it's not that."

"I want to stuff my cock up your ass."

"No, you don't. You don't fuck. Right?"

"I'd fuck you."

"Why?" The man swallows.

"I like you." The boy says as he moves his arm faster, hand a fist around his erection.

Amazing how three words redeem him. The man wipes his forehead, feels a smile hovering near his face.

"C'mon, old man, look at me."

He turns his head. The boy is beautiful and ghastly and radiating heat, maybe voodoo as he rolls his hand around the shaft of his cock and thumbs the head then smears the precome right there on the slit, shiny as newly melted candle wax on a cake.

"Come," the man says.

"I'll come in your face."

The man claws the boy's leg through his blue jeans and then feels how his short fingers dig into dangerous lean muscle. The boy sucks in his breath, maybe angry, and then he lifts his narrow hips off the seat. The man inhales room temperature dough and the smell of shoes left under a car seat. Crotch smell. The man bites the inside of his cheek.

The boy says, "I'm going to blow."

The man doesn't fight when the boy grabs the back of his head then angles his hips so his cock points at his forehead. Jet of come on his left eyebrow. Another clings to his temple. Warm. A spongy aroma.

The man leans back, looks at the ceiling, and this is when he floats.

The boy moves beside him. He's removed his T-shirt and leans over and wipes the man's face. This show of tenderness, why would he do it? The man wants to cry. He takes hold of the boy's arm and presses the shirt over his face. The man begins to drown in a sharp sour smell of the boy's skin.

The boy frees his arm. The shirt falls from the man's face. He snaps his mouth open without meaning to and sucks in a breath. He knows this boy. Or did, a long time ago. "Do you remember me?" he says to the boy who sits slumped in his seat.

"What do you mean?"

The man says the boy's name. "I know your father."

"Fuck you," the boy says. He has pressed his body to the car door.

The man starts the car, and the boy yells.

"I won't go back there!"

The man maneuvers the car from the alley and then turns up a street.

"Fuck you," the boy says again. "He hates faggots. He'd hate you."

The man shakes his head, drives a little too fast. "See, what happened is I blew the whistle on him."

"What are you talking about?" The boy cringes against the door. "Who are you?"

"I caught him siphoning company funds, and as a result he got me fired because, you know, he had all the power, and I didn't."

They approach the corner now. "Please," the boy says, "just let me out here."

The man sees him tremble. He shouldn't leave the boy on this corner again; he knows that. He stops the car, then reaches for his wallet.

"Forget it," the boy says and starts to get out.

"Please," the man says. "Take it, Aaron."

Funny about a breeze, how it can blow dust in a man's eye, and he blinks trying to fight crying as the boy looks at the money then reaches for it before closing his fingers around not so much the money but the man's hand.

Stan Kent

From Here to Indecency

IT IS A PECULIAR CONVENIENCE of the summer weather in Los Angeles that on most evenings following a baking hot day a particularly heavy cooling fog rolls into the Southern California coastal towns providing a thick blanket of mist under which to hide a multitude of sins.

On this one particular night, visibility was cut down to a few feet making it quite difficult for Nancy Thorne and Andrew Benjamin, a phone sex couple on a blind date, to find each other. Since Andrew had called Nancy's phone sex company, Naughty Messages, they had enjoyed sex over the phone for many months and had now decided to meet and have sex in person, on the beach. Both were shy, retiring, rather heavyset people who felt they didn't fit in with the beautiful people of Southern California. That they had found each other through the wonders of modern sex-technology was a sign to both that they were fated to come together in the fog where physical beauty was muted and all indiscretions could be forgiven.

After disturbing several heavily engrossed couples in various stages of copulation, Nancy and Andrew collided with each other at the end of the pier, crushing the identifying white carnation worn by Andrew. Over small talk and nervous laughter he and Nancy plucked the remaining petals and let them fall over the side of the pier into the ocean, the fog obscuring the carnation's fall into the gently rolling surf below.

Or so Andrew and Nancy thought; the petals were interrupted in their flight seaward by the naked body and surfboard of Moose, the legendary nighttime nude surfer of Manhattan Beach. Moose had spent the night, as he did every night, at one of the many surfer bars getting pleasantly juiced until closing time when he'd carried his beloved surfboard down to the water, stripped bare-ass naked, and prepared to surf sans clothes until sunrise spoiled his cover. At which point he'd usually find an alley in which to sleep through the day to prepare for another night of storytelling and drink consuming. He had no money, and he needed none. He lived on the beach—a blanket the only roof he ever needed. He never had to buy a drink—people waited in line to buy him drinks. He ate well—there was always some gullible babe willing to buy him dinner. Moose was a living legend, an icon of indecency that aspiring beach bums, wannabe surfer dudes, and buxom beach chicks all gladly patronized.

Moose looked the stereotypical surfer dude. He was skinny and tanned a deep golden brown. His stringy platinum blond shoulder-length hair was bleached whiter than white. He owned few clothes—shirts of surfpunk bands he'd supposedly been in, a pair of torn jeans—and he never wore shoes. Moose's speech was peppered with the lingua franca of surfing, but unlike many of the poseurs that littered the surfer bars, Moose had earned the right to speak the speak, walk the walk, talk the talk, and surf the surf—naked.

Surfing for Moose was a religious experience, and by surfing naked he felt he communed with his "godhead." Isolated by the fog, in total darkness, he felt like a fetus in the womb. As he crashed onto the beach it was like being reborn all over again. He would get sexually excited by the exhilaration of riding a wave. Sporting a mammoth hard-on of mooselike proportions, he would jack himself off as he surfed, attempting to climax as the wave crashed, leaving him momentarily suspended in midair, ejaculating into the night.

And so when white carnation petals landed on his body and his surfboard he took this as an indication that it was going to be a very special night—and the carnation petals must be a type of manna from heaven sent by the godhead of surfing. So like any good surfer with no money he ate what was offered to him, said "Thanks, dude," burped, and paddled offshore to wait for a really big one to come along—and he wasn't just thinking wave size.

Up on the end of the pier Andrew and Nancy's conversation was stilted. They knew they'd come here to fuck in public, on the beach, as they'd talked about so many times on the phone, but like some difficult to start chemical reaction, they needed a catalyst—and talking about the fog just wasn't going to get cunt wet and dick hard. Fed up with waiting for shy Andrew to make his move, Nancy drew upon Hollywood for inspiration.

"Being by the beach and hearing the waves always reminds me of *From Here to Eternity*. I just love the scene with Burt Lancaster and Deborah Kerr making love in the surf. I see movies like that and it just makes me want to fuck and fuck and fuck. Would you fuck me on the beach—with the waves crashing around us like in *From Here to Eternity*?"

It was all Andrew could do to contain his excitement with his shy, English reserve.

"It would be my pleasure to take you by the sea, amongst the waves."

Andrew offered Nancy his hand, and they ran down the steps to the sand, stepping over a few fucking couples who paid them no attention. They stood before the waves, watching entranced the foaming white effervescence bubbling out of the gray panorama. It was a mystical sight. Nancy ran to the waves to get her toes wet in the ocean. Andrew lagged behind, enjoying watching Nancy dabbling in the surf and lifting the hem of her long ankle-length black dress out of the water. Occasionally a heavier wave crashed, catching her unaware, getting the soft black sweater material soaking wet. Once, one larger wave soaked her to the waist. She squealed like a little girl and skipped away from the water. The wet dress clung to her ample figure, outlining the voluptuousness of her frame. Andrew felt his dick stir harder as he watched her large thighs rub against each other as she ran away from the ocean and then turned and walked back down to the waves, her large buttocks rippling underneath the soaked material. He wanted her with a lust that surprised him with its intensity. In a classical sense Nancy was not a true beauty but there was something fundamentally erotic about the way the wetness of her dress displayed her ample flesh. He wanted to fuck her, he wanted her quickly, and he wanted her forever and he wanted her now. He wanted to plow into her with the force of the crashing waves, just like Burt Lancaster did to Deborah Kerr in the movie.

Throwing his usual embarrassment at being overweight and out of shape into the fog, Andrew stripped naked and followed Nancy into the water. He stroked his dick to keep it hard. The water was freezing cold and definitely not conducive to maintaining a throbbing erection, but he focused on the stimulus of Nancy's soaked form just a few feet away. Just as he reached her she turned to face him. The black sweater dress was sodden and her breasts were on display through the cloth. Andrew reached out and grabbed her tits pulling her toward him by the nipples.

"I want to fuck you here—in the water."

"Oh, God—yes—yes."

Nancy reached down to the sopping hem of her dress and pulled it up above her round belly. The dress clung persistently to her legs in a slinky, sleazy fashion, revealing inches of flesh in a slowly tantalizing striptease as she pulled the hem higher. She'd worn no underwear under the smooth material of the sweater dress because she really didn't own any frilly little panties that she considered sexy enough for the moment. Consequently, the splashing waves had soaked her mound with the cooling saltiness of the ocean, as if the pounding surf had known that inside her pussy she was boiling with lust.

Andrew put his arms on Nancy's waist, holding her as firmly as possible by her swelling buttocks. Fighting to keep his balance under the irregular onslaught of the ebbing tide he bent his legs slightly so that he could enter the rotund woman's sex. It was a difficult maneuver requiring Nancy to guide Andrew's throbbing cock with one hand while opening her cunt lips with the other at the precise moment that Andrew straightened his legs. It took several frustrating tries until the timing was perfected, and Andrew enjoyed the sensuous glide of warm pussy over his cold, hard, saltwater splashed cock. In celebration of his achievement, Andrew wasted no time in thrusting repeatedly into Nancy's moist opening as they stood ankle deep in the icy cold Pacific Ocean. The bulkiness of their bodies made it near impossible for them to stay vertically coupled, and in their lust-charged frenzy to have sex amidst the rolling waves they toppled first one way and then another. The sand shifting beneath their feet made it difficult to stay fixed in any one location, and inevitably the rush of a crashing wave took their legs from underneath them and they fell into the cascading waters. Andrew fell on top of Nancy, the water cushioning their heavy fall.

"Oh, yes—yes—yes—it's just like in the movies. It feels so good."

Nancy may not have been Deborah Kerr, and Andrew certainly wasn't Burt Lancaster—and Manhattan Beach wasn't Honolulu—and the Pacific Ocean in Los Angeles was a darn sight colder than the waters in Hawaii—but it didn't matter. Nancy and Andrew's embraces were the real, urgent, and in glorious glowing Technicolor embodiments of that classic old black-and-white movie fantasy.

Aided by the buoyancy given their bodies by the ebb and flow of the waves, Nancy locked her legs around Andrew's lower body and thrust her cunt at his groin with all her might. The crashing waves buffeted their fucking bodies to and fro, adding overdoses of sexual energy to their already fever-pitched lovemaking. Underneath his thrusting form Andrew was captivated by Nancy's head turning and twisting from side to side as his cock buried itself deep within her quivering cunt. Fucking in the ocean was difficult because the salt water removed every trace of their natural lubrication the moment their thrustings produced that deliciously musky nectar. Each long stab of his shaft hurt immensely as the salt water stung their grinding flesh, but there was no stopping the rhythm of their bodies. The very discomfort they felt drove them on to new heights of sexual excess; to stop would have been even more painful.

Nancy screamed with every searing thrust of Andrew's cock. She writhed underneath his heaving body as if possessed by a maenad spirit. In her long black sweater dress, which was soaked through and pushed up around her waist, she was abandoned to the emotions of raw, primitive sex. With her lying on her back her large breasts had fallen to her sides, pressed close against her body by the weight of her soaked dress. Andrew was captivated to see such mammoth sacks of soft flesh rippling and shaking underneath his thrusts in a way that those of a woman of a much smaller frame and firmer body could never do. He bit hard on her jiggling mammaries. The saltwater-soaked black material covering Nancy's tits intoxicated him with its taste, as if he were devouring a rare caviar or other aphrodisiac. He was able to balance his thrusting weight on Nancy's round belly, thereby freeing his hands from supporting himself so that he could gather up Nancy's breasts and push them together into one huge mountain of flesh. He buried his face deeply into the soaking mass of contrasts—hot flesh—cold water—hard nipples—soft material—salty taste—and feasted, making Nancy scream with a passion that frightened Andrew.

"Oh, fuck—fuck—that feels so good—plunge into me deeply—make me come in waves—like the waves—make me come."

Afraid he was hurting Nancy, Andrew slowed only to be slapped on the back and spurred on with jabs of her legs.

"Don't slow down—don't slow you fucker—fuck me you fucking good fucker."

The words were screamed as if they were the last words she would ever speak. As soon as Andrew had resumed his momentum he felt Nancy's hand underneath his crotch woman-handling his balls. She squeezed the distended sac the way he'd manhandled her breasts. It was agony—and ecstasy—he too began to moan as the fingers milked his orgasm from him.

Fate then dealt its mysterious hand.

Deep within the earth's crust, miles below Nancy and Andrew's fucking bodies, layers of rock, perhaps sensing in some unfathomable manner the release of sexual tension above it, began to pulse and slide, releasing years of pent-up energy. By most seismic standards it produced a small earthquake—the kind California feels almost every month—but in its application—and its ramifications—it could not have been better targeted.

Seismologists at the California Institute of Technology in nearby Pasadena pinpointed the epicenter of the quake as being just slightly offshore of the Manhattan Beach pier. This served to minimize the effects on land, but as a result, the shifting of the sub-oceanic sands caused a rather large wave to erupt where previously only small bathtub-size disturbances had been. The earthquake occurred just as Moose was beginning another run. He was convinced that tonight's surfing was a lost cause when the ocean seemed to fall from beneath him and he was lofted skyward on a thin wall of water.

This was going to be the ride of his life; his erection grew to its normal mammoth mooselike proportions. He stroked the swollen flesh as he plummeted toward the beach. When this wave broke he would be airborne—flying—he would come as he crashed back down into the water to be bashed around in the seething foam of the ocean—his jism mingling with the ocean he so dearly loved.

"A—w—e—s—o—m—e," he yelled into the foggy night, relishing every moment of this once-in-a-lifetime ride.

In their orgasming frenzy neither Andrew nor Nancy felt the earthquake, heard Moose's cry of exhilaration, nor even saw the onrushing wave with the long-haired blond denizen perched precariously on the crest, on top of a fluorescent pink surfboard and sporting a monster of an erection, bearing unwittingly down upon them. As the wave crashed around Nancy and Andrew they were lost in the throes of their release, screaming at full pitch as Moose crashed toward the beach, his cock in hand, desperately pumping away to achieve his own orgasm, oblivious to the passionate couple writhing in his way. Like an automated erotic-homing missile he zeroed in on Nancy and Andrew, his statuesquely hard penis pointing the way, his brain completely unaware of the target before him.

Upon reflection neither Moose, Andrew, nor Nancy had any idea what happened, and neither did the residents of Manhattan, Hermosa, or Redondo Beaches who years later still talked of the bloodcurdling yells that ripped through their half-sleep shortly after the earthquake had disturbed their slumber that foggy summer night a long, long time ago.

The whole act lasted but a few instants, but to the participants it seemed to take an eternity. Moose, ten-inch hard-on in hand, fell on top of Nancy and Andrew's writhing lovemaking as the wave crashed on top of them. The crashing mini–tidal wave threw Moose headlong into Andrew's thrusting bottom at precisely the moment Andrew was sticking his snow-white buttocks in the air, preparing to thrust mightily into Nancy's shaking body. Moose hit Andrew hard, his swollen member penetrating Andrew's humping bottom with one perfectly targeted bull's-eye of a shot. Moose screamed as he orgasmed, his cock suddenly swallowed into the tight constriction of Andrew's asshole. In unison Andrew screamed as he was violated, adding to the primal rush he felt as he orgasmed inside Nancy, and the shocked woman screamed a banshee-like wail that deafened the two others as Andrew pushed harder into her than any single human could. Locked in this bizarre coupling they remained, being washed around the beach like a huge piece of seaweed.

It was quite some time later that they disentangled their bodies, introduced themselves, and pieced together the improbable series of events that had brought them together. Like people who had survived natural disasters or other trying moments, the chance coupling of their bodies forged a bond between them that was going to withstand the strongest test of time.

It was daylight before they could even walk again, and then with some great difficulty. Gingerly—Andrew, understandably, most gingerly of all—they retired, arm in arm, supporting each other to the close by safety of Andrew's house in Hermosa Beach. Over the next few months they forged an unusual *ménage à trois*, and as much as anyone in Los Angeles ever does, they all lived happily ever after—from here to indecency.

THOMAS S. ROCHE

DEATH ROCK

I SUPPOSE I SHOULD BE EVEN MORE FREAKED out than I already am: he's got some pretty weird obsessions. But after a full year with no nookie, I was prepared to agree to anything, and "anything" is what I got. I don't exactly think it's perverted. But I'm not sure anymore whether it's normal.

I was a mournful child. I spent my months, even years, obsessed with death, just like Loren. I don't think you can grow up anymore without thinking a lot about it. Death screams at you from every TV commercial, from the news, from every billboard, and the alternative's not too appealing anymore, either. And when it's not death, it's sex. I spent my time, age sixteen, sitting on the floor in my bedroom smoking clove cigarettes and blowing the smoke through the window; listening to the Sisters of Mercy and Bauhaus on headphones at top volume everywhere I went; dying my hair black, painting my face white;

even using a dagger to carve a cross into my flesh at one point. I was a deathrocker. I ate little and shat even less. I grew emaciated. I wore deaths'-head rings and dime-store rosaries. I fantasized about being a vampire and sucking the blood of those I slept with. I dated a mortician.

But the rings turned my pale skin green; I eventually got hungry; the mortician smelled like embalming fluid. I gave it up, but something remained that made me attracted to Loren—Loren the Depressed Deathrocker—and aroused by him. There was more to it, though: he had a certain creativity, and a passion for loss, that intrigued and fascinated me and touched some deep part of my soul. I fell madly in love with him.

After we had lived together for a year, Loren slipped into the depression to end all depressions. Nothing new, I suppose, for either of us, but along with the other symptoms was a distinct loss of, er, libido. I hate to sound selfish, but I thought I would fucking go insane. I tried everything I could come up with on our limited budget—bubble baths, lingerie, porn flicks, even getting the depressed bastard so wasted on 'ludes that he could hardly say no. But he was unreachable, uninterested; he told me it wasn't me, it wasn't my fault, it wasn't my problem. Bullshit it wasn't my problem!

After a solid year of Loren sleeping next to me wrapped in his garments of black, with his boots on, I finally resorted to my last and final weapon. All the sex books say it's what you do if your significant other is not expressing his significance. I asked him what turned him on.

Sometimes, you don't want to know.

I suppose it's not the worst perversion imaginable, and at least he's willing to tell me his fantasies. But acting them out can get a bit taxing.

It has its erotic value for me, to be sure, but after a while I kind of lost interest. Luckily, the scenario doesn't require me to express much of anything, least of all interest.

He prepares my bath and then makes himself scarce while I don the requisite makeup. I disrobe and enter the bath, trying not to make too much noise. I've gotten used to the sensations by now, and it's really nothing too awful. Except when the ice cubes wedge themselves into unsavory places.

I immerse myself until just my face is exposed, so as not to damage the makeup. I breathe through my nose, with my eyes closed. I used to shiver, but eventually I have learned to control it. I suppose it's bad for my heart, but it's integral to Loren's scenario. I stay in the red-tinted ice water just as long as I can stand it, and Loren knows exactly how long I can stand it.

When the gong sounds, I grow still.

He enters, wearing his garments of black. My eyes are closed at this point, and I do not move. I've gotten very good at remaining absolutely still.

Loren kneels beside the tub, touches my blackened eyes, my white cheeks, my blue lips. He strokes my brittle hair. Sometimes he weeps. That creeped me out at first, but I try to ignore it.

He lifts me out of the tub, and I remain limp. The heat of his body is not enough to warm me, but it feels very good. He carries me into the bedroom, where the heat from the furnace is intense, and my skin feels that much colder. Organ music blares from the stereo. He sets me on the mat and lights the candles that surround it. He gently lifts my head and places a rosary around my neck.

I lie still as he proceeds. I am always glad to feel the heat of his body and of his desire, excited to feel him inside me. But I do not move. I do not stir, not even an eyelash. I have spent months perfecting that; I find that the more I concentrate on remaining perfectly still, the more fervor Loren expresses. Loren is an excellent lover in these cases, I have to admit, and his knowledge of my body is intimate. He plays me like a cadaver flute. Or more accurately, a harmonica.

I remain silent, still, dead, even at the moment of my orgasm.

Sometimes afterward he lets me take the lead, and sometimes he responds a little. But the second time is always for my pleasure alone.

I thought, at first, that it was a temporary obsession, a weird little quirk that would get him off a few times and restore his interest in me. Instead, I found that his obsession grew, and before long he encouraged me to take some 'ludes before the bath, so that my consciousness would be even less. That gave the whole experience a nice rosy glow, but overall I really didn't prefer it. But if I left an open, empty pill bottle on the bathroom counter, Loren's arousal seemed to double. The night I left a razor blade, covered with stage blood, on the edge of the tub, he became like a cat in heat.

Sure, it's weird. It's fucking bizarre, actually. But like I said, I was getting pretty tired of eating pizza and watching TV while Loren lay on the floor, staring at the ceiling, his rosary clutched in his hand. I'd rather be dead, every couple of days, than have a corpse in the living room.

Loren's even started to paint again. Of course, all he paints are corpses and gravestones and the occasional cross. But what the fuck? There have, I suppose, been worse perversions in the history of humankind.

I scratched my nose, and all hell broke loose.

Loren leapt off of me, screaming. "Holy shit!" he said, staring at me as if I was, well, a corpse. He was breathing hard, and not just from exertion.

"What are you freaking out about?" I said, instinctively remaining still and moving my eyes to follow him. "I had an itch on my nose!"

"You're not supposed to do that!"

"It was a hell of an itch!"

"Damn! You scared the shit out of me!"

"All right, look, I'm dead, okay? I'm dead. Watch!"

I lay still, my eyes open wide, my blue lips slightly parted, my cold flesh still.

"No, no, it's not the same. I'll never get back in the mood now."

"Hey, this is getting really weird," I said. "I'm getting kind of freaked out here. Are you going to expect me to really commit suicide some day—just to turn you on?"

He hesitated, then looked very uncomfortable. "No," he said nervously. "Of course not."

"Shit," I said. "I don't think I like that answer."

"I can't do it now," he said, defensive, turning away. He waved his hand at me as if I were a piece of moldy bread. "The mood's been spoiled."

I got up and reached for my robe. "All right, then. Have it your way. Fuck your sick fantasies." I headed for the kitchen to see if there was any pizza left.

Of course, he outlasted me. I'm cursed with an overactive sex drive, so before a week passed I was back in the bath, and Loren was more interested and more demanding than ever. I worked on my meditation techniques. He worked on his nerves.

It went on like that for quite some time, and Loren grew more frightening and more obsessed. I guess after a while, I was able to deal with his obsession more efficiently. I turned it into my obsession. I liked being dead. The closer I was to the big sleep, the more Loren got turned on, and the more I enjoyed myself. I got very good at death.

His paintings improved, too. He still only painted corpses and graveyards—but once, when he was in a very good mood, he dashed off a ghost. I thought that was a profound sign of progress.

It was almost like being sixteen again, except neither of us was depressed. I found myself seeking out ways to make Loren's fantasy more realistic.

I still had my connections to the old scene, and my friends weren't stupid kids. They were drug connoisseurs. I talked to an old boyfriend of mine, and he turned me on to something that just might do the trick. It was some sort of designer drug used for some obscure purpose, but he was able to get me some. It sounded perfect, and I was sure that Loren would approve.

He was coming home late that night, so I drew the bath myself, rose when my flesh was sufficiently cold, lit the candles, set the scene. I took the pills John had "prescribed," and lay on our futon as they took effect. I experienced a strange catatonic pleasure. I was aware, but motionless. I could not feel my heart.

My ears began to ring. My eyes remained open, and watered a little.

Loren's shock was astonishing. His weeping seemed real. I would have risen, then, to make sure he was all right, even if it freaked the hell out of him. That, however, was no longer an option.

He undressed with a cold kind of reservation. I could just see him out of the corner of my eye. I was scarcely aware of my body. I seemed to be floating. He wept as he touched my cold face and my blue nipples.

His mouth was hot, then, and his hands fierce. I could have moaned in pleasure, but that wasn't an option either. It was as if he'd gone insane with desire. He touched me all over, turned me on my belly, stroked my hair, bit my lips, hard. My orgasm was astonishing but still, I did not, could not, move.

Loren lay atop me, weeping, his hot tears running down my face. He teased my tongue out of my mouth and kissed me for a long time.

I was frightened. The afterglow of our lovemaking, if you could call it that, had faded; it had given way to a cold, terrified agony. Loren's tears grew warmer.

He got out of bed, and got my robe. Slowly, ceremonially, he put the robe around my limp body and tied it in front. He sighed, kissed me a few more times, and went into the bathroom.

He drew a bath.

I tried with everything I had to force myself to move. I could not. I lay still as Loren entered the bathroom.

I heard him rummaging through the medicine chest. I heard him splashing lightly as he entered the bath.

Oh, Jesus Christ, I thought. I tried to force my mouth to move, my lungs to work, my throat to scream to stop him. I prayed. I hadn't prayed since Catholic school.

Oh, God, Loren, don't—

It must have been the stress that did it. I faded. There were no dreams.

I awoke with a grim sort of paralysis, a stiffness in my joints, a crashing headache, a cotton mouth—death had given me the worst hangover in the fucking world.

I stumbled off the bed, crawled to the bathroom door, managed to stand. As I moved, my hangover faded a bit.

"Oh, Loren," I whispered as I saw him.

I suppose I expected it, from the very first. Oh, fuck it, there's no use in philosophizing now. I knelt beside Loren, and looked into his open eyes. His mouth was not, as I expected, twisted; his face was not ravaged by fear.

He had a strange sort of peace about him. He looked very happy.

I felt a rush of love for Loren, for his sick obsessions, for his mournful works of art—including his own death, which he had longed for and possibly, in some twisted way, engineered. I smiled and kissed his cold lips.

I looked down at him, at the pale, thin body through the haze of red. I kissed his lips again.

And once more.

I ran my fingers through his hair, surprised at myself.

He was much bigger than me, but he wasn't very heavy. I reached in and lifted him out of the tub, cradling him in my arms. I carried him to bed and laid him down, arranging his limbs just so and brushing back his long black hair.

I took his hand and looked down at him for a long time. I kissed him again on the lips, a full kiss this time, a kiss of heat and desire and love.

I slipped off my robe and let it fall to the floor.

ALISON TYLER

MILK AND HONEY

"INDECENT."

"Excuse me?"

"That's positively indecent."

I couldn't understand what this stranger was talking about, or the way he was staring at my cup of plain black coffee with visible distaste on his handsome face. But I didn't mind him talking to me. He had long dark hair the color of the java in my cup—a shiny, shimmery brown—and glittering gray-blue eyes, like an animal's at night. When he stepped closer to me, he moved with the silent grace of an alley cat. I'd been all by myself a moment earlier, and then magically, he'd been at my side.

"You can't drink your coffee black," he continued, forcefully leading me over toward the counter holding the creamers and sugars—rough raw brown squares, packets of granulated white, pink rectangles of sickly-sweet Saccharine, and an amber-hued honey bear. I registered the choices, but focused instead on the rush I felt when his hand touched my arm. He hadn't taken my hand, but gripped me firmly above the elbow, leading me with a force that took my mind on instant, dirty trips.

"I like black," I said slowly, regarding the array he was offering without considering adding any one of the sweeteners to my cup. I was talking about more than my coffee as I said the words. I meant my clothes, the long ebony skirt I had on today, black cashmere turtleneck, glossy leather boots. And I meant *his* clothes: black vintage concert T-shirt, dyed-black jeans, shiny black shades hanging from the lip of his tee.

But the man wasn't willing to let me off so quickly. If I wouldn't add the sweetness myself, he had another plan.

"Try this," he insisted, holding out his own paper cup.

Sipping a stranger's drink in the middle of the coffee store felt indecent. Savoring the cream in the coffee and honey—my God, *honey*—was something I never had experienced before. Something I would never have imagined.

"Indecent," I said softly, echoing his opening word with a smile, a smile he returned, his teeth flashing sharp and shiny. Once more, I didn't mean the coffee. I meant the way he was looking at me, and the naked promises I saw, stories I read in the moonstone eyes of a stranger.

What he wanted from me was indecent, as well. I shook my head, long hair spilling around my face, swish-soft on my flushed cheeks.

"Let me, Chelsea," he insisted, on his knees now. My clothes were on the floor around us, a slick spill from an oil truck, spreading out on the Berber carpet of my office floor. The door was closed. The shades were drawn, and I was undone at ten A.M. on a Monday morning.

I could hear the bustle of the workers in the offices around us, and I thanked my hardworking frame of mind that had won me my own office at twenty-six years old. Nobody else my age had their own space. But would I keep it if my bosses ever discovered what I was doing behind the closed door?

Not on your life.

Yet that didn't stop me from putting my hands on the cold gray wall and allowing Jonah to part the cheeks of my ass, licking between. Round and round. He pushed me apart, spreading my cheeks like pillows, soft and pale.

"I could put my head here and sleep for hours," he said. But we both knew that he didn't want to sleep. He wanted to spread me open. He wanted to climb inside. He darted his tongue forward, and my knees buckled.

I couldn't think, couldn't speak, couldn't believe that this stranger—I had met him only minutes before—had somehow convinced me to get naked for him. To take off all of my clothes while he watched, nodding with approval from the corner of my desk. That he had managed to make me think this was acceptable behavior for two people who had only just met in a coffee shop around the corner.

Where were my standard rules? Get a man's number. Call after a few days. Set up a date in a safe, well-lit place. Tell your best friend where you'll be in case something goes wrong.

And now?

Now, I was naked, and a man whose last name I didn't even know had his tongue in my asshole. I shuddered, feeling how wet I was, and Jonah responded by pulling my cheeks apart even wider, now sliding one finger inside of me, then two, fucking me with his hand. He didn't ask if I was turned on. He didn't ask if it was okay to touch me like that. He had sized me up correctly in that coffee shop, knowing somehow that I like my coffee black and my asshole licked.

And only when I was ready, only when he had my pussy dripping wet without ever once touching it, did he move to the next step, tearing open a stolen packet of honey with his teeth. Spreading the golden honey on his finger. Skating his fingertip around my asshole.

Indecent: that word appeared in neon letters in my head before the power grid in my head flickered and my mind shut down. Only his tongue was important. All I needed. His firm hands held my cheeks apart, and he licked away the sticky honey. My own palms grew slick on the cold plaster, between the Georgia O'Keeffe calendar and the tiny window overlooking an alley. Oh, if he kept moving his tongue like that. Jesus, God, just like that, I would come.

Without him touching my clit at all.

"Indecent," Jonah said slyly the next day, at the coffee shop. "The amount of noise you made."

We hadn't planned to meet, but there he was. Same exact time as the previous day. I had wondered if he'd be there. I had hoped. When he'd left my office the morning before, he hadn't said a word, hadn't asked for my number, hadn't offered me his. But there he stood, as if knowing I'd be there, as if we'd entered our plans together in our electronic date books.

He had two cups for us, all ready. Cream and honey in both. And he had something else, a roll of duct tape around one wrist.

"I was sure that someone was going to hear you when you came," he told me, handing me a cup of coffee before dropping the tape into my leather hobo bag.

My eyes widened. I looked at the silver-matte of the tape, looked at him, swallowed hard. I could hardly take a sip, because of the heat. We went back to my office once more, with me stumbling over the explanation that I had a, um, meeting, yes, that's right, a meeting with this, um—

"Mr. Miller," Jonah grinned, and our ever-aloof receptionist gave me a nonchalant shrug and went back to talking to her boyfriend on the phone.

So now I had a last name to go with the first, and Jonah had my willing wrists bound with duct tape and my mouth covered with a length of it in moments. I wondered what else he had in his pocket, but I didn't have to worry.

There was honey.

Plenty of honey.

Enough so that this time he dribbled the packet over my pussy, rubbing the honey into my petal-pink folds before searching out every last drop. And then, he flipped me once more, bending me over my own desk, and spread two more packets of the sweet liquid amber around my asshole.

Oh, God, I thought. *Oh, fuck.*

But the words were only in my head, no way for me to say them aloud.

Jonah licked me clean before fucking me, fucking me to the scent of coffee, to the smell of clover honey in the air.

My world changed, then. I went from always expecting the worst, to starting to look for the best. I didn't wear black every day. I added bold red. Bright pink. Colors that signified the way I felt each time I saw Jonah waiting. He had shown me what could happen by adding honey. My whole palette changed, my tastes broadened.

We couldn't go to my office every day. But we found ways. My car. His pickup. A unisex bathroom at the back of the coffee shop. He scouted locations for us—the alley behind my office building. A corner of the big-box bookstore where nobody ever went.

And every time, he had a new way to play, something I'd never done, something I never would have thought of. He blindfolded me in public, in the corner of that bookstore, telling me that people were watching while he undid my blouse. He used clothespins on my clit, slipping his hand into my panties to adjust the device, pinching me so tight I thought I would cry, or scream, or come. He jacked off into a cup of coffee in a doorway while I watched, and then brought me out to a park bench across from the post office to watch me drink in the bright sunshine.

Some afternoons, he surprised me, showing up unexpectedly at my office. He knocked with his elbow. Hard, hard, short, short. Like a Morse code, a made-up language along the lines of the one he had to use at Starbucks when he ordered, two grande, double-espressos with cream.

And honey.

"Don't you work?" I asked him finally, as he taped my wrists to the steering wheel of his car.

He grinned and nodded. "Yeah, of course. Just keep odd hours. That's all." And he told me about his shifts at the grocery store: early mornings when deliveries arrived; leaning against the concrete wall of the store while tasting cherries, biting into a fresh summer peach. The sky like pale purple velvet right before the sun came up.

For two weeks, we were together every day. If we didn't ever meet up at night, I didn't have time to worry about that. Or wonder. I was too well-fucked to care. But on the second Friday, I took myself out for a drink to my favorite corner bar, where people knew me well enough to comment on my new look, to compliment my change of attitude.

The bartender was still the same whiny bastard as always. But Zack knew my tastes, never made fun of me for drinking coffee at night. He brought me a standard mug, black, as always, then complained about his upcoming vacation. Only he would find a two-week trip to Hawaii something to bitch about.

"Indecent," he said, and I glanced up from my coffee, curious. I hadn't asked for milk yet. Or honey. I didn't want to cause a stir.

"What is?"

"The hour I have to get up tomorrow. Six is the number of the devil, you know?"

"Only when you put three of them together," I teased. I liked this blond bartender. He was all California cool, with his hair pulled back in a ponytail, and his tight choker made of tiny shells. Not sexy, not to me, but fun to banter with.

"Eight would be so much more doable. But the flight leaves at nine, and you know the policy. Two hours ahead of time for check-in."

"At least you don't have to wake up that early every day," I said.

"Bartending does have its perk hours," he conceded wryly.

"I know someone who has to be at work at four," I told him, liking the way it felt to talk about Jonah when he wasn't around. Liking the way it felt to think *My boyfriend,* even though I didn't say the words aloud. He hadn't said he was my boyfriend. Not yet. But what else could he be? He brought me coffee each day. Shut the door to my office. Played those dirty little games with me. Honey on his tongue.

"He works at the grocery on Emerson..." I continued, catching my own reflection in the mirror behind the bar. I glowed beneath the artsy bar lights. Shimmered.

"At Dirty Foods?" Now Zack was the one teasing. The store was famous for its organics, but it wasn't called dirty foods. "I know a few people there. Who is it?"

"Jonah." Honey on my tongue this time. The way his name tasted in my mouth.

"Oh, Jonah..." the bartender nodded. "I know Sera."

"Sera?" I asked, setting down my coffee. Bitter now. I'd grown unaccustomed to the taste.

Two knocks on the door, and then two more. Just like before. Just like every other time. But this one was different. Because this one was the last.

Still, I hurried from the desk and turned the knob, letting him in, seeing his grin first, two cups of coffee in his hands. His smile faltered when he caught the expression on my face. His smile fell when he saw my eyes.

"What?" he started, but he knew. "Who?" he said next, but I shook my head. There were tears in my eyes, even though I'd spent the weekend crying, spent the weekend thinking I was over him. Why was I wrecked? I hadn't done anything wrong. I hadn't known. All I knew is this: I'd never drunk coffee with honey before. Never considered anything but straight up and black.

Jonah introduced me to the taste.

So many tastes.

The taste of milk and honey.

The taste of duct tape over my mouth.

The taste of sleeping with a married man.

Jonah handed me the coffee and then turned away. I watched him go, feeling crushed inside, but knowing that I had been a trespasser in this foreign location. I hadn't been meant to stay. I closed my door, and set the coffee, untasted in my garbage. From now on, I'd stick to black.

In the land of milk and honey, we could linger for hours.

In the land of milk and honey, Jonah didn't have a wife.

ABOUT THE EDITOR

CALLED A "LITERARY SIREN" by *Good Vibrations*, Alison Tyler is naughty and she knows it. She is the author of more than twenty explicit novels, including *Rumors*, *Tiffany Twisted*, and *With or Without You* (all published by Cheek), and the winner of "best kinky sex scene" as awarded by *Scarlet Magazine*. Her novels and short stories have been translated into Japanese, Dutch, German, Italian, Norwegian, Greek, and Spanish.

According to *Clean Sheets*, "Alison Tyler has introduced readers to some of the hottest contemporary erotica around." And she's done so through the editing of more than thirty-five sexy anthologies, including the erotic alphabet series published by Cleis Press, as well as the *Naughty Stories from A to Z* series, the *Down & Dirty* series, *Naked Erotica*, and *Juicy Erotica* (all from Pretty Things Press). Please drop by www.prettythingspress.com.

Ms. Tyler is loyal to coffee (black), lipstick (red), and tequila (straight). She has tattoos, but no piercings; a wicked tongue, but a quick smile; and bittersweet memories, but no regrets. She believes it won't rain if she doesn't bring an umbrella, prefers hot and dry to cold and wet, and loves to spout her favorite motto: "You can sleep when you're dead." She chooses Led Zeppelin over the Beatles, the Cure over NIN, and the Stones over everyone—yet although she appreciates good rock, she has a pitiful weakness for '80s hair bands. In all things important, she remains faithful to her partner of more than a decade, but she still can't settle on one perfume. Visit www.alisontyler.com for more luscious revelations or myspace.com/alisontyler, if you'd like to be her friend.